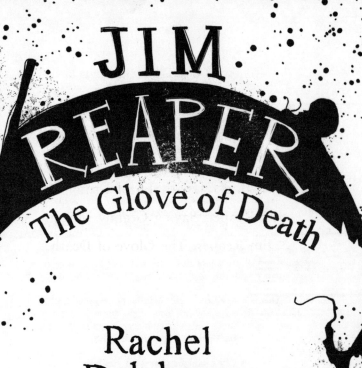

JIM
REAPER
The Glove of Death

Rachel
Delahaye

Illustrations by
Jamie Littler

PICCADILLY
PRESS

First published in Great Britain in 2017 by
PICCADILLY PRESS
80–81 Wimpole St, London W1G 9RE
www.piccadillypress.co.uk

A CIP catalogue record for this book
is available from the British Library.

ISBN: 978-1-84812-587-2
also available as an ebook

1

Typeset by Palimpsest Book Production Limited,
Falkirk, Stirlingshire
Printed and bound by Clays Ltd, St Ives Plc

Piccadilly Press is an imprint of Bonnier Zaffre,
a Bonnier Publishing company
www.bonnierpublishing.com

For Billy B-F and Sophie G.

How I Knew My Dead Babysitter Would Be Okay

Life isn't easy when your dad is Death. Yep, that's what I said – my *dad is Death*. Didn't you know?

Perhaps, like the rest of the world, you thought he was Terry Wimple, Senior Accountant at the Mallet & Mullet accountancy firm? Nah, that's a cover-up. He's the Grim Reaper. And I suppose that actually makes me – Jim Wimple – Jim Reaper, son of Grim. So now you know the truth, are you curious to know more? *Exactly*. So was I.

Whenever the coast was clear, curiosity took me to my dad's study, which was very much out of bounds. My favourite thing in there was a book called the *Death Dictionary*. I always had to lift it down from the bookshelf with two hands because it was so heavy. It was enormous, too, with a dark-leather cover, all dusty, and the pages inside were thick and waxy. It had strange words and definitions. For example, there was:

Human Existence machine (a machine that selects Clients) *and*
Clients (people who are ready to die) *and*
Trouble Clients (people who are ready to die but aren't giving up that easily) *and*
Deaths (people who bring about death – there's more than one of them).

A lot of what I read I already knew, from

overhearing Dad's phone conversations and from the secret fact-finding missions I'd carried out at The Dead End Office, where Dad works in town. There, I'd come across men and women in dark cloaks, scribbling deathly information in giant registers. I'd walked through spooky corridors and passed doors with names that made the hairs on the back of my neck stand up – names like the Brain Training room and the Glove room. I'd never had time to stop and investigate the many strange rooms and corners of The Dead End Office, as my missions were always done in a bit of a hurry. But that's exactly where the *Death Dictionary* came in handy. All the details were right there at my fingertips.

And speaking of fingertips, there was one day when I needed to know about a certain single white glove. It sat in a box in Dad's study when he was home, and he took it with him when he went to work. I was pretty certain it wasn't a fashion item and my curiosity was burning a hole in my head. So I looked it up in the *Death Dictionary*. This is what I found:

GLOVE OF DEATH

A Glove of Death is coated on the outside with a death-inducing substance. A single touch is enough to bring about death. When putting on a Glove of Death, the other hand must be protected to avoid touching the Glove of Death with bare skin, and causing a self-induced Mishap. See MISHAP.

Naturally, I freaked out. I mean, a Glove of Death? In our house? A deadly weapon disguised as a winter accessory? After I discovered that, I steered clear of Dad's study for a while and also kept a distance when he was rushing out the door, in case the glove flew out of his pocket and deaded me on the spot.

But after the initial shock, my curiosity crept back in, loaded with questions. Questions are like that, aren't they? You start off with a couple, find the answers, and then suddenly there are thousands more. My best friend Will would say questions are like snail eggs, huddled together, hatching one after the other. But that's typical Will, and you'll discover more about him and his snail obsession later.

What started the ball rolling, or the question eggs hatching, was the mention of Mishaps.

What were Mishaps? I turned to the page in the *Death Dictionary*.

MISHAP

When a death is carried out that has not been approved, this is a Mishap. Mishaps can be reversed and life returned to the victim of the Mishap using the Mishap Procedure, which can only be administered by a highly trained Correction Team. See **CORRECTION TEAM.**

Wow. WOW!

It's weird enough finding out that your dad is a death do-er with a deadly white glove. But to discover that the dead can be brought back to life? I never for a moment thought I'd find out something as crazy as that. But I'm glad I did. Because if I hadn't discovered that death could be undone, then imagine how much I'd have freaked out when I killed my babysitter.

That's right. I killed my babysitter. I didn't mean to. It was 100% accidental.

Chapter 1

But let's go back to the beginning. Back to when my little sister was making me choose gruesome ways to die. For Hetty, this is normal dinnertime conversation.

'Jim, if you had to die, would you rather sink slowly into a swamp and drown or be catapulted so high into the air that there was no more oxygen and you suffocated?'

'Um. Pass.'

'That's three passes, Jim, so you have to

answer this one. You absolutely *have* to. Ready? Jim, if you had to die, would you rather freeze to death or be stung to death by bees?'

'Hetty!' Mum gasped. 'Just eat your cauliflower fritters.'

'He has to choose, Mum,' Hetty said, digging her heels in and definitely not eating her cauliflower fritters. In fact, I saw her slip one off her plate, drop it on the floor and kick it under the table.

'Stung to death, please,' I sighed.

'Okay then . . . but I warn you . . .'

'Warn me, what?'

'That bees' stings take four days to kill you and the venom attracts ants and flesh-eating beetles that will try to eat you while you're dying.'

'You didn't mention that. Frozen alive, then, please.'

'Okay, but you'll be freezing to death in a

see-through ice machine, naked in front of your whole school.'

'That's stupid,' I said. 'You never gave me all the information.'

'Life never gives you all the information, stupid. Nothing is straightforward. You need to learn that.' She shook her head pityingly, which in turn shook her bouncy fringe – another thing that wasn't straightforward. It was cut at a wonky angle. Hetty cuts her own hair because she says all it takes is a hairdresser who's into horror movies and you could lose an ear.

'No, life isn't straightforward. Not when *you're* around, Hetty,' I laughed.

'Mum, would you rather die of an exploded tummy after eating too many lentil burgers or from being poisoned by radioactive algae?'

'I'm not playing this game,' Mum said huffily.

Mum's idea of conversation was more

informative than existential (which my best friend, Will, told me means 'being alive and stuff'). She preferred to discuss the benefits of listening to Mozart, and eating mung beans. Preferably at the same time for a double-whammy of goodness.

'Where *do* you get your algae from?' Hetty peered at Mum's drink, with a curious frown.

'Nowhere contaminated,' Mum snapped. She cleared the plates away without even noticing how little Hetty had eaten. My little sister knows exactly how to get out of eating Mum's terrible food.

If you haven't met my mum before then I have to tell you – she's a bit of a health nut. If she heard me say that she would say, 'I'm simply interested in wellbeing, Jim, and you should be, too' and then she'd list the health benefits of eating nuts. She owns an online health-food shop called The Happy Husk. The latest craze at The Happy Husk headquarters (our house) was algae pulp, and she was putting it in nearly everything we ate. She said it was the best thing ever, but every time Mum finds a new superfood it's the 'best thing ever' and holds the secret to happiness or good sleep or better bowel movements. I wish she wouldn't talk so much about that.

'It's *natural*, Jim!' Mum laughs whenever I wrinkle my nose. Everything natural is good, apparently.

But Mum, despite loving everything natural, doesn't like snails.

I don't mean *escargots* like the French have with garlic butter. I mean she doesn't like them at all, full stop. Not in her dinner, and especially not alive and well in her vegetable patch. Spiders, ants and everything else in the garden – yes; snails – no. If she did like them, maybe I wouldn't have ended up killing the babysitter.

But I'm getting ahead of myself. Because before my life got infinitely more complicated thanks to Mum's dislike of snails, I simply asked her, after dinner, a very, very simple question.

The question? Would she buy me a DVD. That's all. And this was the answer:

'If you want to rot your skull, I won't be helping you to do it. You can be responsible for your own lobotomy, Jim.'

'Yeah, Jim,' Hetty chimed in. 'Would you rather die from falling down an elevator or from eating too many lobotomies?'

Hetty clearly didn't know what a lobotomy was, but I'd read about it in my *Gruesome Science* book. It's an operation where some of your brain is scraped away. Sometimes it scrapes away a bit of your personality too. It sounds horrible!

Mum had got it into her head that televisions

emit vicious electronic waves that have the same effect on the brain as a lobotomy. You might agree if you saw Will watching *Spongebob Squarepants* – his mouth hangs open and he goes all limp, as if the giggly yellow sponge in the cartoon has absorbed his entire being; it's a pretty good impression of something that existed long before monkeys. But Will's an exception. For nearly everything.

When I'm watching TV and Mum asks a question and I don't reply, it's because my brain is just too busy digesting information. How can I stop to think about whether I've emptied my lunch box in the middle of trying to work out how Dr Who remotely calibrated his on-board computer from another dimension? Exactly! If you asked someone a question when their mouth was too full of sandwich, you wouldn't say that person had forgotten how to talk, would you?

Anyway, I only wanted the DVD of *Percy Jackson*, which I think contains interesting and educational information about the classical mythological gods, combined with action and adventure. I was hoping Will would come around to watch it with me. He was scared of programmes with proper people and more than three characters, but I was hoping to broaden his horizons.

But Mum had made up her mind. If I wanted the DVD, I'd have to buy it with my own money. The trouble was, I only had 40p.

But I had an idea.

I rejoined her in the kitchen. She was blending strawberries, flaxseeds and green pulp from a packet. Dried algae, probably.

'What's that?' I asked as sweetly as I could. She turned the mixer off.

'I'm experimenting with a new concoction,'

Mum said, 'and it doesn't have a name yet. But it's very, very good for you. Do you want to try some?'

Without waiting for my answer she poured it into a glass. Well, it didn't really pour – it kind of bellyflopped in one solid splodge.

'Here,' she said, holding it up to the light. 'Get some of that goodness into you, and then you can make up a name for it.'

'Okay!' I smiled (I had to get on her good side), and knocked the glass back as quick as I could, letting the gloop slide down my throat. I tried not to be sick – for the sake of Mum's feelings, and for the sake of getting a DVD. From the corner of my eye I saw she was nodding and grinning, eyes wide, waiting for my verdict.

I gargled uncomfortably. 'How about calling it Berry Slime?'

'Berry *Sublime*. Yes!' she cried. 'You are a clever cookie. Well?' she insisted, now almost panicky with excitement. 'What does it taste it like? What's it like?'

I was so horrified by the texture I could barely talk. I gave her a thumbs up.

'Oh, marvellous!' she cried. 'That's vitamin C, fibre, and in that packet is the goodness equivalent of one kilogram of vegetables. Incredible, isn't it?'

'Yeah, incredible,' I gasped. 'What's it made of?'

'I'm not sure,' she pondered. 'My yoga instructor gave it to me. What a lovely man. So connected with the Earth, you know. Like me.'

'Er, Mum, now that I've had a healthy boost, I was wondering if you had any jobs I could do for you.' I wrapped my arms around her waist and squeezed tight. 'For money,' I added carefully.

'Watch it, Jim!' she scolded. 'I'm standing in perfect symmetrical alignment. You'll throw me off balance!'

'Please, Mum.'

She softened, but only facially – her body stayed very much aligned. 'Well, all right, there is something you can do.'

'Anything!' I said, happily.

'You can do something about those bloomin' snails in my vegetable patch.'

She wanted them gone. Dead. And she would give me 10p for each one.

10p a snail wasn't a bad rate. Especially when there were loads of them. And after a quick glance under the leaves of Mum's pumpkin plants I could see there was more than a DVD in it. If I made good time I could probably even afford to buy the whole *Percy Jackson* box set, and a bag of salt 'n' sweet popcorn too. But there was one problem.

This may sound weird, considering who I am – the son of Death – but I'm not all that okay with killing things. Not at all.

Chapter 2

I'm not like my best friend, Will. I don't think snails are the most awesome thing to slide across the face of the Earth. But I think they're alright.

For a start, they're not that slimy. They have a muscular foot that ripples, pushing them along, and a scratchy lip called a *radula* that chews up food as they move over it. I know all of this because Will gave me a crash course in snail anatomy once, even though I didn't ask for one, which was nice. But those feelers and eyes and the way they poke in and out – you have to admit they're epically cute. And they don't do any harm. They just eat stuff in the garden. How are they supposed to know it's Mum's organic veg patch they're scoffing? All in all, I'm in favour of letting snails live.

But here was my dilemma. DVDs cost quite a lot more than I had. And I really, really wanted that DVD because it had been a while since I'd bought any new films. And let's face it, Mum would kill the snails anyway . . . But killing them by stamping on them, like Mum suggested, seemed a horribly vicious choice of execution. Especially coming from one so connected with the Earth. And I wasn't going to sprinkle salt on them like some people do; Will said it pulls all the water out of them which makes them panic and produce frothy slime until they kind of implode and explode at the same time. Urgh!

There had to be other ways to kill snails.

How would you rather die, snails? I thought to myself. *Be smashed to death or . . .*

Or what? I didn't know. But I knew someone who might.

When I got to Hetty's room she was standing on a box in front of a fan, turned on full blast. Her arms were in the air, and her head was thrown back. Every few seconds she moved into a different position. Her hair and clothes blew around wild and crazy-like.

'What are you doing, Hetty?'

'I'm being a wind artist,' she said. 'See how many different artistic angles there are?' She turned her back to the fan and her hair flew up in front of her face.

'I have to ask you a question.'

'I am only accepting wind-related questions today,' she said, bending over so her skirt blew upwards, inside out. It's okay, she was wearing dungarees underneath. Hetty never dresses traditionally.

'It's not wind-related. But I will give you some

money.' No response. 'MONEY, HETTY,' I shouted over the roar of the wind.

'Oh, right!' she said, hopping off her box and turning off the fan. 'Why didn't you just say so!'

Hetty likes money. She likes it a lot. She 'collects' coins she finds lying around the house. She says it's because she doesn't want them to be lonely. But I know the money goes right into a special hiding place in her room with all the other lonely money for a very good reason. She's saving up for a horse. Or scrounging up for a horse, more like. She's not afraid to ask for money. Even the postman has donated to her horse fund. I think it's because she stood on his feet and wouldn't let him leave until he did.

'So what is your money question, Jimble Wimble?' she said, rubbing her hands together.

'It's kind of a death choice, with a twist.'

'Twists cost more.'

'I thought they might,' I tutted. 'Okay. The twist is that you're a killer, but you're also a pacifist. That means you don't like hurting things.'

'I can be a pacifist, easy.' Hetty grinned. 'For money.'

'I'm sure you could. Now, here's the question: if you had to kill something but didn't want to hurt it, what would you do?'

Hetty tapped her chin. Her eyes widened.

'I'd get someone else to kill it. Or . . . I'd push it off a cliff. Or . . . I'd starve it.' Hetty looked annoyed as I shook my head. 'Jimble, I've given you three very good answers and now you have to pay up. And pass me that scarf and those gloves. I must practise my wind art before the grand exhibition.'

'What exhibition?' I asked, genuinely confused. I passed her the items.

'The Wind Exhibition. You're not invited. Unless you pay twenty pounds.'

I laughed. Hetty wrapped the scarf around her waist and pulled on the gloves. 'If you,' she said, pointing at me, 'try to sneak into the exhibition uninvited without payment, it's on pain of death.'

I looked at Hetty's gloved finger. She prodded it towards me again and poked me on the nose.

And then it hit me.

'That's it!' I exclaimed, to myself really.

'Pay up,' she said, holding her hand out. I put a twenty-pence piece in it. 'Not exactly a windfall, Jim,' she said grumpily.

'But I came up with my own idea. I'm not using any of yours,' I protested.

'I bet I helped, though. Things don't just come

to you, Jimble,' she said. 'Nothing's ever straightforward.' She reached out and lightly flicked my nose again with her gloved hand.

I gave her the last 20p I had left in my pocket, because actually she was right – she may not have said it, but my devious six-year-old sister with a weird dress sense and a wonky fringe had pointed me in the right direction, and given me a most excellent idea.

I crept into Dad's study and pulled back the black cloth that covered the special glass box that contained the Glove of Death. I wasn't really expecting it to be there. Dad was out of the house, and wherever Dad goes the glove usually goes with him. I know that, because after I found out about the Glove of Death in the *Death Dictionary*, I kept a close eye on it. Well, you would, wouldn't you – a glove coated with a death-inducing substance needs to be watched carefully. You wouldn't want to come across it feeling for money down the back of the sofa. *Ooh, ten pence . . .* dead.

I had never been up this close to it before.

There had never been a situation where Dad wasn't home but the Glove of Death was, because Dad's almost always out doing the sort of work that requires death-inducing; he's a really busy man. He's in charge of Natural Deaths in Greater London, and there are a lot – A LOT – of people in Greater London. There's a printing machine that chugs away in the corner of his study, making a never-ending list of people in the area whose turn it is to *get a visit*. It's called a DADS – *a Direct Action Death System*. Day and night, it chugs on and on and on, letting Dad know whose turn it is next to get the touch of death . . . It sounds ominous and scary, but of all the death jobs, Dad has the nicest – he puts people to sleep, and usually it's very old people. If it was your turn to die, then I would recommend my dad. Dad's a real softie. He'd do it ever so gently, with a feather-light touch of his glove.

And that's what I thought I could do with the snails. Much nicer way to go than any of the other options. With the glove, all it would take was a single touch and it would all be over. Peacefully, gracefully, all over.

The fact the glove was there in his study, and Dad wasn't home, meant that Dad had booked some time off work (his deputy Death would take over). Probably to go trainspotting. He loves trainspotting. I looked in the drawer in the hallway where he kept his train notebook and binoculars – yep, they were gone; so right now he was definitely on a station platform with a flask of tea waiting for some big locomotive or superfast city train with interesting numbers on it to come by. But trains come and go pretty fast. If I was going to stroke those snails to death, I had to do it quickly. There was no time to lose. It was time for a Snappy Meal (I just made that up. Catchy, don't you think?).

I carefully lifted the lid of the box. It lay there, looking no more menacing than a carefully stitched old-fashioned glove – the sort worn by butlers for polishing silver. It didn't look like something that could kill you in an instant; it wasn't embroidered with the word 'death' and it didn't carry a toxic warning sign. It was so ordinary that I almost forgot about its deadly capabilities – I almost picked it up with my bare hands. Luckily my attention was snapped away by something falling off the table and onto the floor.

At first I thought it was the cat, Mr Darcy. We don't know if that's his name, or who he belongs to – it's not any of the neighbours we know. Mum just started calling him Mr Darcy after some character in a book who's a bit moody. Mr Darcy, the cat, is always sneaking in and making himself comfortable in our home. He's jet black and snoozes in the shadows, sometimes unnoticed for hours. He's definitely a bit moody if you try to budge him. But it wasn't Mr Darcy in Dad's study. It was a black glove. There was no mention of any other colour glove in the *Death Dictionary* . . . I reckoned it had to be there to protect the other hand, like the dictionary had said.

With my left hand protected inside the black leather glove, I carefully pulled the white one over my right hand. Mum and Hetty could come looking for me at any moment and I was suddenly very nervous. Beads of sweat popped out all over my nose. With the sweat beginning to create an itch – and knowing that if I scratched my itch with the wrong hand, I could stroke myself to death – I realised that a horrible accident was only ever going to be a fingertip away. I was going to have to be extremely careful.

I took a few deep breaths to calm myself down. Then I made a silent apology to the God of Snails. I don't know if there is a snail religion, but to be safe I invented a God of Snails (*Molluscus Deus*, if you were wondering), and that seemed to help. And now I was ready to kill. As softly as I could.

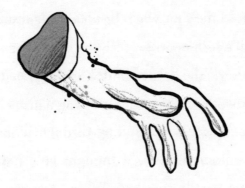

Chapter 3

'Off to get those bloomin' snails!' I called merrily as I passed Mum in the kitchen.

She didn't reply right away. I think some of that Berry Slime Smoothie was lodged in her throat. I stood by just to make sure she didn't choke, hiding the Glove of Death hand behind my back. I saw her throat peristalsis at work – that's when the rings of throat muscles push food downwards, causing a ripple or a gulp.

Will told me that when he was explaining how a snail's foot works.

'Blimey!' she gasped, when she'd managed to swallow the mixture. 'That was a fruity one. Oh, Jim!' she said, smiling through pink-and-algae-coloured teeth. 'I thought you'd started on those snails ages ago. What have you been doing?'

'Preparing myself. Er, with a bit of meditation.'

After all, it was premeditated murder, I thought . . .

'Oh right,' she said, slightly confused.

'I'll be off, then!' I chirped, backing out of the kitchen door in reverse, my right hand held way behind my back at a safe distance. She watched me, baffled. It was attention I didn't want. 'Hey, Mum, why don't you make me another of those lovely drinks while I'm killing snails? I'm sure it'll be thirsty work.'

'I knew it wouldn't be long until you adopted my taste for wellbeing, Jim,' she said brightly. 'I just knew it! I'll whizz you up another one. Just give me two secs.'

Outside, next to the vegetable patch, I dropped to my knees and lifted a large pumpkin leaf. I spotted my first victim. It was *Mum's* first victim, I reminded myself. I was just the deathly messenger. Bit like Dad, I suppose.

The little guy had a yellowy house with a brown line that spiralled round his shell. His body was light grey and slightly see-through. I never thought I'd use the word 'pretty' for anything, let alone for a snail. Even Will's big sister, Fiona, who really *was* pretty, with pretty eyes and pretty dimples and pretty hair, I'd rather describe as *cool* or *awesome* (please don't tell anyone I said that). But this snail was definitely pretty.

Then I noticed loads of them, and how different they all were. There were big old snails with bodies coloured battleship grey – they looked like old army colonels in rusty tanks – and there were tiny pink snails, medium-sized snails with shells in yellows, reds and browns, and with stripes, flecks and camouflage spots. There were so many. But I couldn't sit and admire them any longer. I had work to do. I carefully held out my hand . . .

'Hey, Jim!' It was Mum calling from the back door. 'I'm going to take Hetty into town to do some shopping. We'll be gone a while. Indigo's coming over.'

'I don't need babysitting,' I moaned. Indigo is the daughter of Mum's yoga teacher, and the worst babysitter ever. She's miserable and never talks. She just hangs around like a bad smell.

'I know that, darling, but she just phoned. She's looking for jobs to do this weekend to make some extra money and I said there were enough snails out there to go round. She'll be here in a minute. Dad will be back later. I think he's waiting for the 4.20 train from Stafford. Your Berry Sublime is on the kitchen counter. With added dandelion root, just for you!'

'Okay, thanks, Mum,' I said as cheerily as I could, although inside I was growling about Indigo. I had better get on with it – get rid of as many snails as I possibly could before she got here and made the glove-work impossible.

I looked at the snails but my determination dissolved again immediately. They were so gentle and sweet and unsuspecting. I raised my index finger and held it above the little head of Lemony Fred (alright, so I named him, big deal), ready to send my first snail to sleepy land . . . but suddenly I felt like I was being watched, like a hundred eyes on stalks were all turned towards me, a hundred tiny souls silently screaming 'don't do it'.

My hand was shaking.

Get a grip!

I couldn't do it – not to Lemony Fred. In our short time together, we'd become far too close.

I threw him over the fence into the neighbour's garden.

Then I turned my attention to the old battleship, who was almost as big as my thumb, with eyes as thick as floorboard nails. Goodbye, Colonel Bert. Goodbye . . . No! *Dammit!* I'd named him, too, and that made us practically friends. I threw him over the fence.

I picked up Curly Sue. Threw her over the fence.

Little Pickle. Over the fence.

Slippy Dave . . .

Then I started to cry. Not a real crying, just a sob. A kind of groan. Nothing really. I don't know why I mentioned it . . .

Pull yourself together, Son of Death. Pull yourself together, boy . . . There was a creak as the side gate opened and I looked up. Indigo loped into the garden, face covered by hair as she looked down at her mobile phone. She didn't even say hello, or make eye contact. She just grunted in my direction and walked to the other side of the lawn, where she stood gormlessly, leaning on a hip. Good – she was far enough away not to bother me and it didn't look as if she'd be snail-killing any time soon. Her phone kept buzzing.

I turned back to my patch. With my non-gloved hand, I collected all the snails I could find and put them in a pile. Better to kill them all at once, so it was over with as soon as possible, and that way they wouldn't die alone. In the pile, they began to unfurl and crawl on top of each other, shyly touching each other's eyes and feelers. Perhaps they were getting to know each other. Perhaps they were making introductions or chatting, or swapping advice for best eating spots in the garden. Argh! This was making things so hard!

'What are you doing, Jim?'

That sounded like Will . . . Will!

I looked up and there he was, leaning over me. He had a book tucked under one arm.

'Hey, Will. Where did you come from?' I asked nervously.

'From Norwich Hospital. My parents moved to London when I was four –'

'No, why are you *here*, *now*?'

'Oh, you said you were quite interested in squid the other day, so I popped round with this – *The Big Squid Fact Book*. Thought you might like it for bedtime reading.'

'All I said was I tried calamari on holiday and quite liked it!'

'Well, you've got to start somewhere. I'll leave it here,' he said, laying the book at my feet. 'Can't be long. Fiona needs to get home.'

'Fiona's here?'

Fiona – Will's awesome sister.

'Yeah. She gave me a backie on her bike. She's waiting out front and she's seriously impatient. There's a Bruce Lee movie on TV. He's a karate legend . . . Hey, what are you doing there, Jim?'

'Um . . . weeding.'

'Looks to me like you're collecting snails. You've got a few garden snails there, and – look! – that's a lapidary snail, that flat one. I knew you'd appreciate the members of the mollusc family one day, but squid and snails all at once? You're racing ahead. Very cool, Jim.'

'Thanks, Will,' I said, shifting uncomfortably.

'What's that on your hand?'

We both looked at the Glove of Death.

'A glove.' I didn't know what else to say.

'White isn't a great colour for a gardening glove.'

And that was probably one of the most intelligent things he'd ever said since admitting that the nutritional goodness of nose bogies was probably not enough to justify eating them.

'No,' I agreed.

'And you've got a black one on the other hand.'

'Couldn't find matching ones,' I said. And there was silence. That meant Will was thinking.

Will's brain works in really strange ways. If life is a play, Will sees it from backstage, not out front like the audience; ordinary things confuse him, but sometimes he can see through confusing things quite clearly. It's a matter of perspective. And he definitely comes at life from a funny angle. He and Hetty have a lot in common.

'Probably a good idea to wear gloves,' he said finally. 'Because snails and soil carry parasites and microbes, and I know for a fact you don't wash your hands very often. You're actually quite filthy.'

'Exactly!' I exclaimed, not caring about his accusations. I knew he didn't mean it in a bad way.

'What's *she* doing here?'

Will was looking at Indigo, who had put her phone away and was now crouched down and peering into the bushes, much like I was.

'Weeding, for extra money,' I said quickly.

But it turned out I couldn't protect Will from the truth, because Indigo stood up, holding a large garden snail in the air and shouted, '*Got a big one!*' Worse than that, she then turned and looked at me.

'How many snails have you killed, Jim?' she said.

The first time she speaks to me in her whole

life and she has to go and say that – right in front of Will, the world's greatest snail enthusiast!

'What does she mean, Jim?' Will said, staring at me with eyes like giant marbles.

'I'm not killing mine, I'm just moving them,' I stammered.

'No point in moving them. Snails are homing creatures, Jim. They'll just come back home.'

'Well, *I'm* being paid to kill them.' Indigo shrugged and put the snail down on the grass. She raised her foot above it.

'Stop her!' Will cried. 'Stop her.'

If you know me and Will, then you know that there's one thing I hate and that's seeing my best friend upset. He's much more sensitive than I am. And he's especially sensitive about snails. I've seen him retreat to bed for a whole day after an accidental snail death. Seeing one crushed on purpose under Indigo's shoe would be a recipe for a major breakdown. There was nothing for it. I had to stop her. I reached out, and . . .

Chapter 4

'What did you do to her?'

Will pointed down at Indigo, who was
sprawled, flat on her back on the lawn. I held
back the surge of panic that was building inside
me. It raged just above my stomach, making me
feel sick.

'I just touched her,' I whispered. Which wasn't
a lie, because I did touch her – I just happened
to grab her by the shoulder with the Glove of
Death.

'She's dead,' Will gasped.

'No, no she's not,' I said quickly, not sure what to say next. 'She just fainted.'

Will stared at her a little longer, then back at me. His eyes inflated like rising doughballs.

'That. Is. *Incredible!*' he shrieked. But it wasn't a horror shriek, it was an excited one. 'Flippin' chestnuts! *You* did *that*?'

'Er . . .'

'Fiona told me all about the One-Touch,' he continued, nodding at me furiously. 'It's one step away from the Touch of Death, which is the cone snail of martial arts moves.' Will slips a snail reference into most conversations if he can, and I'd heard about the infamous cone snail before. It has a long protruding finger that shoots venomous darts. 'The One-Touch is a temporary knock-out but it's still cool and it's, like, an ancient secret, Jim! Where did you learn it?'

'Er, Mum's yoga teacher,' I said, looking at Mum's yoga teacher's daughter, dead at my feet – by my own venomous white-gloved finger, which I was still holding out. I quickly hid it behind my back in case Will wanted a closer look. But Will (unsurprisingly for Will) had been distracted and was no longer looking at Indigo, me or my deadly finger. He was looking just past me up the garden, and had started making a revolting sucking noise.

'Why are you making that noise?' I asked him.

'Cats are attracted to it. Cats are very curious creatures. Watch.' Will made the noise again, and I looked round to see Mr Darcy had approached us, his tail flicking. Then Will shrieked. This time it *was* a horror shriek. Mr Darcy had begun toying with the large garden snail that Indigo had dropped on the lawn.

'Do something, Jim!' Will said, not for the first time. 'Do a One-Touch on the cat!'

'Why don't you just pick up the snail?' I said crossly.

I was suddenly overwhelmed by the number of people and animals in the vicinity, dead and alive, and the dawning realisation that I would be in a whole world of trouble if I didn't do something about it.

'I can't. It'll scratch me. Look at its claws – they're like fishhooks! I'll get an infection. One-Touch him, Jim!'

'For heaven's sake, Will!' I growled. I bent down and pushed Mr Darcy away from the snail with my gloved hand.

But did Mr Darcy fall over as stiff as a cardboard cat with his tongue sticking out and his legs in the air? No, he gave me a filthy look and then stopped pestering the snail so he could lick his bottom. Will swooped in and plucked the traumatised snail from the grass.

'The One-Touch clearly doesn't work on cats,' he said. 'Probably because cats' bodies are different to human bodies. It's all about pressure points, isn't it? Isn't it, Jim? There probably is a cat-specific One-Touch if you understand cat anatomy. I could point out pressure points on a snail . . .'

I let Will talk about snail acupuncture for a few seconds. It gave me the opportunity to peel off the glove and shove it in my pocket, and to gather my thoughts.

'When will Indigo wake up?' Will was looking back down at her, stroking the snail in his hand, and gently smiling like this was the best day ever. He hadn't noticed that Indigo didn't seem to be breathing.

'In about five minutes,' I said with a confidence that came from nowhere.

'I'd better go,' he said, and I sighed with relief. 'Fiona will be getting cross and you know what that means!'

I did know what that meant. When things don't go her way, Fiona can be as cruel as a cornered Viking.

'I can't wait to tell her about your One-Touch, Jim,' Will said, walking up the garden. 'She's totally into martial arts at the moment. She's going to be so impressed.'

Awesome Fiona? Impressed with *me*? If ever there was a cloud with a silver lining, this had to be it. Although, as I watched Will disappear back through the side gate and out of sight, the cloud positioned itself right above my head. And it was very dark indeed.

I was alone with the terrible truth – I'd killed my babysitter.

At this point, you might be wondering why I wasn't curled up in a ball, blubbing like a baby or screaming in panic – after all, Indigo wasn't just One-Touched, she was *dead*. But funny things happen when you're in shock. I was eerily calm, like a proud and loyal sea captain at the wheel of a sinking ship. And despite being dead, right there and then Indigo looked kind of healthy. Like a Sleeping Beauty, just passing time until a prince came to give her the kiss of life. With Indigo's rotten attitude, it would have to be a bloomin' saint that gave *her* the kiss of life . . .

But I knew in truth, if anything was going to bring her back to life, it was going to be the *Correction Team*. Because this, my friends, was a *Mishap*.

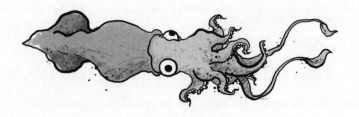

Chapter 5

I pulled the *Death Dictionary* down from the shelf and found the page I was looking for. The page that would make it all okay. This is what it said.

CORRECTION TEAM

The Correction Team is the term given to the group of workers at The Dead End Office that deals with Mishaps. The Correction Team, given the time and *location of a Mishap, can visit the scene of the Mishap and return to life those that have mistakenly met death. See **MISHAPS**. Refer to the **Death Protocols** manual.*

So that was it! All I had to do was give the Correction Team the time and location of the Mishap. It was simple. But then again, it wasn't really all that simple. The Correction Team was at The Dead End Office.

This was no time for nerves or for questions (because we all know questions only multiply). I had to get down to The Dead End Office and reverse this Mishap. The trouble was, I couldn't do it on my own. I needed help.

I jumped on my bike and pedalled like crazy, hoping I could catch up with Will and Fiona. Luckily, they had stopped at the top of my road to talk. Will was prodding Fiona's shoulder with a pointy finger, and weirdly Fiona wasn't retaliating. Usually with Fiona it's *touch-me-and-you're-dead*. I'd seen Fiona fight, and it wasn't a pretty sight. Well, it kind of was, but you know what I mean.

'Hey!' I called, and they both stopped. Fiona turned to me.

'Hi, Jim,' she said. 'Nice to see you.' That threw me. Last time I saw her, Fiona had said that the sight of pathetic slugs like me and Will made her feel sick.

'Hi, Fiona,' I said, blushing a little. 'Will, I need your help.'

'There's a Bruce Lee movie on TV in a minute. Do you want to come over?' Fiona smiled so hard her dimples appeared.

'Um. That's a nice offer,' I stammered, 'but there's something I need to do. Will, I need to sneak into Dad's office.'

'What for?'

'Er, um . . . it's a secret.'

'A secret mission?' Will asked.

'Yes, something like that.'

Will said he had to pop home for provisions, but he met me outside Shakalaka Milkshake bar fifteen minutes later, as planned. I brought my walkie-talkies. He brought a large backpack,

which he explained contained everything we might need for a covert mission. Oh, and he was also wearing a black cape and a red cravat. He looked like a miniature vegetarian vampire.

'What are you wearing, Will?'

'I have come as my alter ego, Will-Magico.'

'Will-Magico?'

'Yes. I have decided to borrow survival tricks from the animal kingdom to turn me into a stealth magician. Perfect for the tasks of hunting and surviving. And therefore, secret missions.'

'It's a bit ridiculous, isn't it?' I laughed.

'Coming from you . . .' he said, grumpily. He had a point. I was wearing one of Mum's Happy Husk T-shirts, which said: *Organic Fruit Ninja*.

'What's in the bag?' I said, changing the subject.

'I have notebooks, pens, binoculars, measuring tape, camera and a sound machine.' He pressed the button on the sound machine that made a balloon-pop noise, followed by the one that made a gun-shot sound.

'What do we need that for?'

'Distraction and deception are the pillars of animal trickery,' Will said, nodding wisely. 'For instance, the fork-tailed drongo makes meerkat distress calls so the meerkats run away and the drongos can eat their food.'

'Brilliant, but we're going into town.' I smiled. 'Not foraging in the Amazon.'

I'd told Will that I was arranging a surprise birthday party for Dad, and we were popping into Dad's work at the accountancy firm called Mallet & Mullet to talk about it with Dad's secretary, Susan, with the chipped tooth (she broke it eating one of Mum's rock cakes). Will would never suspect I wasn't telling the truth because he doesn't understand lies. His brain is dense with facts. There is an occasional air bubble of silliness, but definitely no room for anything else. For that reason alone he was absolutely on board with his role in the expedition – to stand guard outside and alert me if Dad or anyone else turned up, using the walkie-talkies. I don't like taking advantage of Will's trusting nature and I absolutely hate lying to him, but I'd told him the truth about Dad before and it only led to sticky situations that got stickier than one of Mum's honey-mushroom pancakes with date-syrup topping.

We pedalled as fast as we could down the main road that led from our neighbourhood into town. Will talked about the speed of squid – he was determined to expand on my experience of calamari, which was fine, although trying to keep calm while maintaining top velocity on my bike was taking all of my concentration.

When we pulled up outside Mallet & Mullet, Will had turned a bit grumpy.

'You weren't listening to a word I said,' he whimpered as we dismounted.

'I did, Will,' I lied. 'Every word.'

'Like what?' he challenged.

'You said the word "the" a few times.'

I knew 'the' was the most common word in the English language. I also knew that Will's brain would automatically accept that as a valid answer, because it was true.

'Fair enough, Jim,' he said. 'I think I did say *the* colossus squid is *the* largest mollusc in *the* sea.'

'Okay. So, let's go.'

We walked through the sliding glass doors into the pristine marble-floored entrance hall of Mallet & Mullet accountants. It was all for show. Because behind the foyer, I knew there were crumbling corridors and ancient doors belonging to the building's real business – The Dead End Office, the place where people's death dates are decided, logged, arranged and, fingers crossed, reversed.

'This way,' I said, pulling Will towards one of the foyer's huge potted tree-ferns. We slid behind it into the small space between the pot and the wall and lowered the leaves so we could see the foyer clearly. 'This is perfect. Stay here and don't move. Every time someone walks in, let me know on the walkie-talkie. Even if it's not Dad.'

'But why?'

'Because . . .' *Er, yes. Why?* 'Because we should take the opportunity to make this a fun and exciting game. And I want to feel like a spy.'

I'd feel an idiot saying something like that to

anyone else, but Will doesn't judge. It's hard to know exactly what he was thinking, but it wouldn't have been *my best mate's an idiot*. It's likely he was thinking about the elasticity of slug slime compared with the stretchiness of melted cheese. With Will, you never can tell.

When the coast was clear I crept back out from behind the fern as quietly as I could. I had to turn back and tell Will off for playing with his noise buttons. He apologised and retreated into the foliage.

I looked at the smooth marble walls around me. They were covered with grand pictures of famous landmarks – the Eiffel Tower, the Golden Gate Bridge, the Taj Mahal. But I was looking for the landmark that wasn't man-made. From previous investigations at The Dead End Office I knew that of all the images on the foyer walls it was Mount Fuji that was special

– not only was it a natural landmark, it was the trigger that opened the secret sliding doors that led into the creepy passages beyond.

I spied it on the wall opposite. I looked left and right, then left again, and sped across the floor, skidding to a halt and flattening myself against the wall. I sidled up to the picture. I tilted it. There was a click, and a door right behind me slid open. Bingo!

I stepped in, the doors closed, and the gloom swallowed me up. My eyes took time to adjust to the bad lighting, but I already knew I had no idea where I was.

The picture of Mount Fuji had been in a different place every time I'd been to the offices. It had opened a different secret door to the one I'd been in before, leading to a new area in the maze of corridors behind. This wasn't helpful. The place was like a rabbit warren, riddled with passageways and offices with strange signs and weird functions. On all the walls dusty portraits hung – faces of previous workers at The Dead End Office.

The first time I went there I came across Dad's portrait; he was painted in a serious pose, with piercing eyes looking down his nose. It was as if he were about to give someone The Cold Eye (I'll tell you about that later). It sent shivers down my spine, but not half as much as the pictures of some of the more ancient Deaths, with their strange-shaped skulls or old-fashioned hats or crinkled faces with missing teeth. Death had been around for a long, long time. Even as the son of Death, I felt mighty small.

The corridor I stepped into now was a new one, and it didn't have faces on the wall. Instead there were framed newspaper articles, all of them about unexplained deaths and unsolved murder cases. Headlines shouted *Mount Everest Tragedy* and *River Rapids Take Five*. It was a wall of Misadventures work. I knew all about Misadventures. The special team swoops in and brings about death to those in pain, to save them from even more pain. It's not for the faint-hearted. The stories on the walls here were so tragic – the Misadventures team must have risked their own safety to make sure those people didn't suffer for too long. I stopped to look at a faded parchment with hieroglyphics and a drawing of an old woman on top of a pyramid. I wondered, briefly, if she knew she was going to die and tried to get closer to heaven. Or perhaps her family put her there, trying to get her as far away from Death as possible. It reminded me of how I once tried to save Will's granny. I tried to get her as far away from Dad as possible. But it wasn't that straightforward, as it turns out.

Just then there was a crackle and a desperate, whispery voice.

'Two men approaching Mount Fuji. I repeat. Two men approaching Mount Fu– They're in, Jim! They're in!'

I pressed the button on the walkie-talkie. 'Thanks, Will.'

I needed a hiding place. I turned circles looking for a door. I pressed my ear against one labelled *Quills*. There was no sound, so I slipped in.

Inside were boxes and boxes of brand new feather quills and, on the wall, cabinets displayed old ink-stained ones – not all feather; some were sharpened sticks, some were reeds. The quill was the king of communication in The Dead End Office. Nothing was written on computer. Everything was scrawled and scratched in leathery tomes. The quills in the cabinet had tags alongside – a name tag with the names of the Death workers they had belonged to. It was a curiosity treasure trove. I would have stayed and devoured the history of it all, if only I had more time! But I absolutely had to ignore the interesting rooms; there was only one I needed: The Correction Team.

When the footsteps had passed I peeked out from behind the door. The two men were still ahead of me in the corridor. I held my breath, but they were walking quickly – they seemed to be in a rush – and I watched their black cloaks billow behind them like squid ink in water. I wondered what their jobs were. Were they administrators, glove-makers, Deaths? But I was getting distracted by pesky multiplying questions again. And distraction was the downfall of a man on a mission; distraction in the animal kingdom could get you caught.

Quickening my pace, I ran round three corners and down some stairs and into a basement area where I came across a landing with three doors. One of them was what I was looking for. *Correction Team* was the door on the left. *Mishap Detailing* on the right. *Toilets* in the middle. I quite needed the middle door at this point, but I needed the Correction Team more urgently, so I slipped a note with the details of the babysitter mishap under the door and ran. Job done.

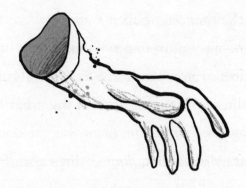

Chapter 6

I had to retrace my steps. The last thing I wanted was to get lost in the corridors of The Dead End Office. If I did, then:

a) my chances of getting caught would rise considerably,

b) the chances of Will losing patience would rise considerably,

c) the chances that Will would come looking for me would rise considerably,

d) the chances of all the above
      happening in one evil cluster of
      misfortune would rise considerably,
   e) oh, and I might just lose my mind.

I went up the stairs, turned three corners – a left and two rights, just the way I'd come – and then along a bit, and – **crackle.**

   'Jim!'

   'What is it, Will?' I hissed, breaking into a run.

   'Another thing. You said you wanted to be a spy. Well, did you know squid are not only the kings of distraction, they are also the masters of disguise and they have a protein called reflectin that makes them almost invisible? Kind of like magic. A lot of magic is to do with tricks of the eye.'

   'Is there anyone coming?'

'*No.*'

'Don't communicate unless it's to let me know if anyone's coming.'

'*Okay.*'

There was a sudden ***boing boing!*** – like a kid playing a kettledrum.

'What was that? Are you being bopped on the head? What's happening?!

'*It was the falling-down-the-stairs button. Pressed it by mistake.*'

Usually, I'd have found that a little bit funny, at least, but I was in trouble. My mind had been taken off my route and forced to think about squid proteins and staircase accidents.

And I was lost.

I thought the last corner I'd turned would put me back in the corridor with the newspaper articles. But on the walls of this one were pictures of Deaths. A Native American Indian with red-painted cheeks glared at me with a scowl so deep his craggy face looked like a mountain range. What was I going to do? I could retrace my steps and risk going wrong for a second time, ending up lost even further in the deepest bowels of The Dead End Office, or I could keep going forward and hope that I came to an area of the office I recognised.

The clock was ticking – for Will's patience and for my patient, Indigo. I imagined her lying cold on the ground, all alone and deaded, and I shook with the horror of it. But with any luck she'd soon be in the hands of the Correction Team. They would make everything right again.

I ran through more passageways and past countless doors, and then, finally, I came across a room I knew. The Boardroom. I'd been inside it before. I'd hidden under a table and listened to a meeting of Deaths, discussing topics like

Trouble Clients and unfortunate endings involving Misadventures, and how to make the numbers work . . . Yes, working out the numbers was something they had to do when too many Trouble Clients were clinging to life. Balancing the ins and outs is the one thing The Dead End Office does have in common with accountants.

As I neared the Boardroom I heard voices behind the door. Ah, that's why the men had been in a hurry. There was a meeting! This was good news, as it meant most of The Dead End Office workers would be inside and the corridors would be empty. But something about it bothered me. Dad was in charge of Natural Deaths. He was one of the leaders – a top Death. A Death that always spoke at big meetings. Why wasn't he here? Why would they have an important meeting on his day off?

Knowing I had no time, knowing it was risky,

not knowing exactly why I was doing this, I put my ear to the door. Behind it vibrated the very loud and crystal clear voice of Mr Sinister, the Chief Officer of The Dead End Office. Dad's boss.

'*Reaper has been in charge of Natural Deaths for too long, now . . .*'

They were talking about Dad!

'*. . . He has been remarkable. An excellent Death. He can do the job with his eyes closed. But when a job becomes so easy you can do it with your eyes closed, then that's when mistakes are made. It's time he rose to the challenge. And a challenge has presented itself. Due to the sad loss of Mr Thanatos, the highest position in Misadventures now needs filling. So are we in agreement that Reaper should be moved to head up the Misadventures Team?*' (A big cheer, then someone said something I couldn't hear.). '*Yes,*

yes, *I'm aware that blood is an issue for Reaper.*' (A snigger.) '*But the team in Brain Training are certain they can help him overcome this. Now, I think it's time for a little break.*'

I heard shuffling, coughing, murmuring. A mention of chocolate digestives. It was tea-break time. Deaths would be popping out to go to the loo. I had to go too (not to the loo).

I ran, zigzagging this way and that way – past Dad's own office with its *G. Reaper* sign on the door, and that of his secretary Susan, with the chipped tooth, and past the General Office, where I could hear the click and whirr of the Human Existence machines inside, churning out names to be sent to all the DADS machines, for Deaths to deal with. And I kind of knew where I was. I was on the right track. I kept running, right until I came to a dead end.

Dead ends don't sound promising, but here

a dead end with no door means one thing: a way out. I nudged the last framed picture on the wall next to me (an Amazonian tribal warrior with green parrot feathers around his neck) and it slid open.

There was a crackle from the walkie-talkie.

'*Jim.*'

'Yes, Will.'

'*There's someone coming.*'

'Will –'

'*He's short. He looks a bit like you.*'

'Because it is me, Will,' I said, parting the fern leaves and making him jump.

'Oh, sacred sycamores, Jim! You frightened the life out of me.'

I told him I'd arranged Dad's birthday surprise and Will didn't ask what the surprise was, which was good. Instead he talked about his own birthday, which he'd been thinking hard about even though it was still seven months away. For his birthday he wanted to stand outside the Houses of Parliament and petition against the importing of escargots to Britain.

'Snails have to be starved for at least two days before cooking. Starved then cooked, Jim!' Will stopped to hiccup back his own despair. 'We can start making banners of protest and getting signatures. We have to stand up to this cruelty against snails!'

After the close encounters I'd had in my own garden with snails I had some sympathy. But the serious face I wore now was for another reason.

Mr Sinister's words played over and over in my mind. Dad was going to be moved to Misadventures! Dad loved his job in Natural Deaths because it was gentle and tender. Disasters and accidents and tragedies, and watching people in pain would be his idea of a nightmare even if he *wasn't* afraid of blood. But he *was* afraid of blood – terrified, in fact. It would take a lot of Brain Training to get rid of that.

The Brain Training Team was in charge of all sorts of weird brain stuff, like mastering mind over matter – it's how come Dad knows how to wipe memories (and I'll tell you more about that later). But memory wiping was a skill, a brainy bonus. This time they wanted to take something away that had been lodged in Dad's brain since forever. They'd have to dig deep to get rid of his fear of blood, and what would that involve? Vicious electronic waves, like the ones Mum was scared of? A lobotomy? Would Dad ever be normal again? Would he turn into a bloodthirsty killer? Would he still like *Mr Bean* and jokes and trainspotting? I couldn't let this happen.

For a day that started with a sticky situation, this was getting more treacly by the minute. But I had to tackle one thing at a time. I had to get home and see if the Corrections Team had sorted out Indigo. Once that Mishap was all cleared up then perhaps I could think of a plan to prevent Mr Sinister making Dad do the worst possible job on Earth.

Chapter 7

Will wanted me to go back to his house to start work on the *Say No To Escargot* banners but saving more snails wasn't my top priority. It was 4.15. Five minutes until Dad's train came in. After that, it wouldn't be long before he got home. I just hoped that the Corrections Team had come and done what they had to do, and Indigo had woken up, got bored and gone home to play on her phone.

I made the excuse that I needed to go back

and check Indigo hadn't resumed her job of snail hunting.

'That reminds me,' he said. 'I told Fiona about your One-Touch. She was so blown away she couldn't speak.'

Although the thought of Fiona being in awe of me was kind of great, I knew deep down that Will telling her about the One-Touch was a bad, bad idea. Lies were a bit like questions – they multiplied. If she asked me how to do it, it would all go very wrong. At best I'd have to admit that I didn't know any martial arts moves at all – not even the basics – and at worst, I'd have to tell Will about the Glove of Death and then about Dad being Death, and I really did not want to go there again.

But right now I had more immediate problems. I was eager to see what was – or wasn't – waiting for me on the lawn. I ran straight through the side gate and into the back garden. There she was, still. Peaceful and undisturbed. The Corrections Team hadn't been. Maybe it was too soon. There was nothing in the *Death Dictionary* to say it was immediate. Perhaps it took days – weeks, *months*!

I freaked out. And probably about time. I stamped up and down and ran around the lawn and screamed. I was cross at them, but most of all I was furious with myself and also a bit annoyed at life. My teachers always talked about initiative and taking responsibility, and I had! I'd tried to show initiative by cleaning up the mess I'd got Dad into before he ever knew there was a mess. But it had come to nothing. Worse than that, it was going to get a lot, lot worse if Dad saw Indigo. Because if Dad saw Indigo I'd have to tell him about the Glove of Death and about sneaking into his study and reading his books and breaking all the rules. Then Dad would never trust me again, and trust is a huge thing between me and Dad. If I broke his trust, he'd kill me. Not literally, I hope. But my chances of being super-trusted number-one son would be right out the window.

What was I going to do? Run around and scream some more, of course.

Just then I heard the back door open and Dad's whistling ('Can't Touch This' by MC Hammer). I stopped, mid-scream. What was he doing back so soon?

'What's going on?' he said, pausing on the doorstep, looking alarmed. He relaxed and smiled when he saw that I was fine. Then he looked at Indigo. 'What's this – game of Dead Lions?' Dad called happily. 'Can I join in?'

Before I could say a word he ran down the

garden and sprawled himself out on the grass next to Indigo. There was a silence that seemed to last forever. You could have heard a snail sneeze.

'She's too good at this,' sighed Dad. 'I'm afraid I can't stay still that long. You see, I'm too excited!' He jumped up and ruffled my hair. 'Want to know why?'

I nodded. What else could I do?

'The train from Staffordshire was a new one. I've never seen it before. Even better, there was no one else on the platform – apart from passengers, that is. So perhaps I'm the first trainspotter to ever have noted it down. Unlikely, but nice to think so, eh?'

'But I thought it wasn't arriving until four-twenty,' I said meekly. 'You're back a bit soon.'

'*Three*-twenty, Jim. It was in the station for

nearly thirty minutes. Got a really good look at it.' So Mum had the times wrong. Dad breathed great happy puffs and then stopped.

'What's up, Jim?'

I coughed a little. 'Um, Dad . . . It's about Indigo . . .'

'She's stupidly good at Dead Lions, isn't she? Remind me never to play with her again!' He shook his head, pretending to be disgruntled.

'No, Dad,' I said. 'She's more than not moving. She's not breathing, either.'

'Good tactics,' Dad nodded. 'When you breathe your chest rises and falls and if you've got a Dead Lions' judge who's a bit picky, they'll pull you up on that. You'll be out.'

'Dad. She's dead.'

'She's a Dead Lion –'

'No. Just dead.'

Usually, good ideas come to me when I'm under pressure, but with Dad's arms wrapped tightly around my head in a heavy embrace – shielding me from the horror on the lawn – it felt as if my head and my heart were exploding.

'How did this happen?' he wailed.

I tried to tell him that I was okay, but Dad just took my muffled speech for sounds of distress and hugged me tighter and tighter.

'Shhh, I'm here, Jim.'

There was no point in trying. I let myself be hugged and waited for Dad to release me. Eventually he did and without saying another word he pulled me into the house and sat me down in the kitchen. He searched my face for signs of traumatisation. I opened my mouth to speak, but he slapped his heavy hand on my shoulder and shook his head, long and slow.

'I've tried to protect you for so long,' he

moaned. 'I've tried to keep work and home life apart, and I don't know how this has happened, but I do know I've failed!'

'You haven't, Dad –'

'Yes, I've failed. You've been exposed to . . . And I had no idea, no idea . . .' he trailed off. 'Where's your mum?'

'She's taken Hetty shopping.'

'Good.' He went to the cupboard at the back of the kitchen and retrieved his secret stash of chocolate biscuits. He balanced a tower of them on the table in front of me. 'You must be in shock. Eat these and stay here. Whatever you do, don't move. I have to make a phone call, but I'll be back as soon as I can, okay? Just keep it together, Jim. Keep it together, son. Keep it together, you hear!' He turned around in circles, drumming his hands on his thighs, clearly not keeping it together.

'I will,' I said softly. 'You'd better make that phone call.'

Dad left the room and suddenly everything seemed really ordinary – just a normal day in the kitchen. I looked around at it, at the fridge, at the piles of stuff on the counter, the overflowing bin and the worktop splattered with slimy Berry Sublime. Without thinking, I dabbed my finger in it and it stuck like glue. It wasn't half as sticky as the situation on the lawn. Because what I had created was well and truly the goo of doom! But I couldn't dwell on my mistakes. Although things weren't exactly great, all wasn't lost yet. Dad just needed to give the Correction Team a kick up the bum and it would all be over, so long as things were straightforward (and I prayed to the God of Almightly Boo-Boos that it would be). The Glove of Death was still in my pocket, and it suddenly felt heavy as a rock. At some point very soon, Dad would find out that the glove wasn't where it should be. I'd cross that bridge when it came to it, because I couldn't put it back now. Dad was in his study.

I knew who Dad had gone to call, and although it's not polite to listen in to conversations, there are times when it's absolutely necessary to be one step ahead of the game.

Dad uses the home phone when he's talking to The Dead End Office. The home phone is a landline – mobiles are too dangerous to use because of hacking, snooping and problems with accidently pressing an app with your chin. As all Death conversations have to be quick and clear, Angry Birds or Fruit Ninja theme tunes would be seriously frowned upon. Landlines also mean that people outside the house can't overhear your conversation. But if you're inside the house it's easy – you just pick up a telephone receiver in a different room. And that's what I did. And this is what I heard:

'. . . appears she may be dead.' That was Dad's voice.

'*What do you mean DEAD?*' said the other voice.

'Well, Mr Sinister, I mean she's not moving or breathing. And she's not playing Dead Lions. She is actually dead. And I need to know if this was some sort of plan that I wasn't told about.'

'*Well, you know very well that the workings of other Deaths are secret – there's no reason you should be told about it.*'

'I know that. But there's no b-b-blood. No sign of an accident. It's just such a shock, and so strange that our babysitter should be taken at such a young age in my own back garden. Could you look into it for me? Please?'

'Very well. Hang on a minute . . . No, there's no record of anything here. Must have been some sort of Mishap.'

'Can you reverse it?'

'You know we don't do that sort of thing lightly . . .'

'But you will reverse it, won't you?'

'None of the other Deaths were in your area at the time. It must be a Mishap closer to home. We won't be doing anything to correct it until you investigate how this abomination happened and give me a full report. The Mishaps Detailing Team need to look at this before we get Corrections involved.'

I placed the receiver down very carefully. You have to, or it makes a clicking sound that can be heard by the others on the line. I'd learned to be careful with that. You wouldn't think punishment for listening in on a phone call would be too bad, but Dad is Death, remember, and he also has the power to hypnotise and make people forget everything they've seen and heard.

I went back in the kitchen and I lay with my head in my arms on the kitchen table and waited for Dad. I imagined that my face might now be showing signs of traumatisation, because behind it my mind was racing at 100 miles per hour. I'd pushed my note under the wrong door! It should have gone to *Mishaps Detailing*. Not that it mattered – *who* and *where* wasn't enough on its own. Dad needed to know *what* had caused it. If I confessed everything now then Dad would be able to give the Mishaps Detailing Team all the information, and then the Corrections Team could get started. But I really had crossed a line by taking the glove. I'd crossed lines before, but as lines go, this was a biggie. Dad would be furious. He'd give me

The Cold Eye, which is the look I told you about. It's where mean meets maniac; it's where his cheeks suck in and his eyebrows sink so low it looks as if they weigh a tonne each. Then he'd wipe my memory to be super-sure that I could never meddle with his job ever again. Then I would think he was a regular accountant for the rest of my life, and the rest of my life would be . . . normal. Like I say, life is hard when your dad is Death, but it is also kind of exciting.

If an idea didn't come to me right away, it would be over. All of it. My life as I knew it. All for the sake of a couple of cute snails and a *Percy Jackson* DVD.

Dad appeared, his phone call finished. He came and ruffled my hair. I looked up at him and he was pale as Death should be. In this case, that wasn't good.

'Dad, did you ring the office and tell them about Indigo?'

'Yes,' he sighed.

'So they'll do something about it, then?' I asked innocently.

'No, Jim. It's not as simple as that.'

Dad walked into the kitchen with his hands in his pockets and his head hung low. He paused in front of me a few moments. His foot was tapping.

'Jim,' he said – quite sternly I thought, but then he did have a lot on his mind. 'Jim, you're going to have to tell me everything that happened today. Everything, from the beginning to the end.'

Oh no. This was it. My ability to think quickly under pressure had vanished.

It was over.

Chapter 8

By the time I'd told Dad about getting out of my pyjamas, putting on my underpants, eating cereal with extra milk (because I like my cereal a bit slushy) and brushing my teeth, he looked a bit irritated.

'Not from the *very* beginning!' he said through gritted teeth. 'Get to the important bit.'

Ah. This was the bit I was holding back on.

I'm normally quite a good kid, so I'm not

comfortable with telling whopping big barefaced lies, but under the circumstances it had to be done, to prevent the breakdown of father-son trust, and to prevent inevitable memory-wiping. 'Well, it all happened in the garden . . .' I said quietly.

'I can see that, Jim,' said Dad. 'But WHAT happened in the garden? What killed your babysitter?'

Here goes.

'Snails,' I said boldly.

'What do you mean – "snails"?'

'It could have been the snails,' I said.

'Snails,' Dad repeated.

'I was collecting snails and, er, apparently some people react badly to them – you know, they carry parasites and cause itching and can make you ill, like prawns, if you eat them and you're allergic to them.'

'Are you telling me that the babysitter was out in the garden eating snails?'

'No . . .'

'Then what ARE you telling me, Jim?' Dad was sounding a bit angry.

'I'm saying that snails shouldn't be underestimated.'

'Have you gone insane? Have you gone stark-raving bonkers? HAVE YOU . . . ?' Dad stopped when he saw my face, which I could feel was going a little red and hot. 'Sorry, son. You've had a shock. You're upset. I shouldn't be shouting at you. But I really do need to know how this tragedy happened. And I need to know as soon as possible so I can put it right.'

My cheeks burned. Dad took a big breath, although I could see he was on the edge of losing his cool, big time.

'Death by snail allergy is very unlikely, and

we should strike it from the list of possibilities. Think, Jim. Think. What killed her?'

I shrugged. What else could I do? Dad started to look at me very strangely.

'Did you have an argument with her?' he asked slowly.

Blimey, he was asking if I'd killed the babysitter!

'No, of course I didn't!'

'It would be quite understandable,' he said calmly, like a police detective coaxing a confession from a villain. 'Perhaps she was being bossy?' he tried.

I shook my head.

'Perhaps she was making fun of you?' he tried.

'No.'

He paced up and down like a mad person waiting for a bus, and there was a silence that went on and on and on. I could see anger and frustration making Dad's face take on the Cold Eye. I hate the Cold Eye more than anything. Even more than Mum's four-leaf lasagne.

Then three things happened at once.

1) I heard a miaow at my feet,
2) I put my hand in my pocket – the one with the black glove (phew!),
3) I had a brilliant idea.

I told you I was good under pressure. And this was serious pressure, as I didn't have much time. As Dad turned away to pace up and down the kitchen I grabbed Mr Darcy, who was rubbing himself against my shoe, and using the black glove I tucked the white one under his collar. Then I gave him a sharp nudge, and he ran away just as Dad turned round.

Bingo!

'It could have been the cat,' I said.

You might not understand how I could blame it on the cat at this point, but trust me, in my mind, the plan was suddenly crystal clear.

Dad's face, which had been twisting into the Cold Eye suddenly stretched into wide-eyed disbelief.

'A cat, now?' he rasped, flabbergasted.

I nodded.

'First snails, then cats . . . Can we stop discussing animals and talk about what on Earth is going on!'

'Well, Mr Darcy came to see us while we were outside.'

'And . . . ?'

'And he was very affectionate . . .'

'And . . . ?'

'And – well, there was one odd thing. There was something white stuck to him. Don't know what it was. Maybe a tissue. Or a . . . looked like a glove of some sort . . .'

Dad suddenly stood very upright and still, like a cardboard cut-out.

'What's the matter, Dad?' I asked gently.

He didn't reply. He turned about on his heels and walked slowly, stiffly, like someone very scared, out of the room. Two seconds later I heard a yelp. I ran to his study where he now stood, hand over his face, body bent double, in front of his desk. On his desk was, of course, the empty glass box. No glove. But there were originally two gloves – and the black one was still in my pocket. I pulled it out gently and let it fall on to the floor by my feet. I kicked it away from me.

'What's that box for, Dad?' I asked.

'It's nothing,' he said miserably. Then he let out a wail.

'Dad?'

'How could I be so stupid!' he cried.

I stroked his back gently. 'Maybe you'd feel better if you talked about it.'

He turned round, his eyes rimmed with red and, to my surprise, he nodded.

'I've wanted to protect you for so long, Jim, but as I'm going to need your help, I'm going to have to tell you . . . Inside this box was a glove. It's a very important glove. More important than you could ever imagine.'

'Is it this one?' I asked innocently, pointing to the black glove on the floor.

'No, not that one. A white one. That damn cat stole a white glove – but the white glove is . . . is . . .' he began to crackle.

'Is it full of death?' I suggested.

He nodded.

'Then we need to get it back,' I said. 'It's okay. Mr Darcy's in the kitchen.'

Or rather, he had been. But the back door was open and he was nowhere to be seen. This situation couldn't get stickier if it covered itself in superglue. I started to feel the colour drain out of my face too.

First, there had been hope: the death of Indigo could be reversed. Second, it wasn't entirely hopeless: things were a bit trickier, but Dad just needed to report exactly what was happening to The Dead End Office. *How was he going to do that!*

Third, it was time to abandon all hope: Mr Darcy was on the run with the Glove of Death.

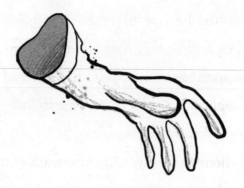

Chapter 9

'We'll get him, Dad,' I said boldly. 'Come on.'
I held out my hand and he took it.

It's funny how sometimes when other people
are feeling bad and helpless, it makes you feel
strong and sensible. I felt like that a lot when
I was with Will – when he couldn't work out
how to open his crisp packet or read the bus
timetable, I got really decisive, really capable.
I was never like that when his sister, Fiona, was

around, though. When she's there, half my brain disappears. I don't know why she lobotomises me. She just does.

Just then, the doorbell rang. I left Dad in the garden and went to answer it.

'Tell them to go away,' Dad wailed after me. 'We need to find that cat.'

Fiona was stood on the doorstep, her hands clasped in front of her as if in prayer, eyes bright and shiny, her dimples blazing.

'Hi, Jim,' she said sweetly.

'Er, hi, Fiona. Will's not here.'

She stared at me intensely. 'Will said you knew how to do the One-Touch. I'd really love it if you'd teach me.' Fiona leaned forward and stroked my arm.

This was insane. She was touching me! Usually Fiona ignores me totally – at best she snarls or calls me pumpkin-head. But I didn't have time for this. I could hear Dad whimpering as he paced around, looking for the cat.

'Not now, Fiona,' I croaked. I looked into her eyes, and slowly closed the door. She stuck her foot out to jam it. This couldn't be happening. She wanted to talk to me – and I wanted her to want to talk to me – but it was really a very bad time. 'No, Fiona,' I said firmly, kicking her foot away and slamming the door shut. I heard a little shout of frustration from the other side. There was a little shout of frustration inside my mind, too, but it was the whine of despair from Dad I was more worried about. I walked out into the garden to help him search for Mr Darcy. He couldn't be far. I took a blanket to lay over Indigo too. In case she woke up or something, or got cold. It didn't seem right to leave her there, all exposed.

'I've always been so careful,' Dad sniffled. 'I've never left the box open before in case – well, in case something like this happened.'

'It's not your fault,' I said honestly. It's the least I could say, really.

'It *is* my fault. You see, I must have rushed out when I heard about the 3.20 train from Stafford. I must have. I must have put my own interests before the safety of my family. Because, Jim, the worst thing about all this is . . . it could have been *you*!' He stared at me and shook his head with guilt. 'My boss is going to kill me!'

'Literally?' I gasped, horrified.

'No, not literally,' he corrected. 'But it's not going to turn out well, even if we do get Indigo back to life.'

'What do you mean "if"?' I asked.

'I've got to give a full report of what happened.

I can't do that until we get that glove back under lock and key, because when you have a Glove of Death –'

'You shouldn't let it out of your sight,' I finished.

There was a miaow from the next door neighbour's garden. Then came a kindly voice.

'There you are, Mr Darcy. I was wondering where you'd –'

A thud. Then silence.

'Quick!' I shouted, and Dad threw me over the fence and followed after.

On the other side we saw the lovely Mrs Dewberry on the ground and Mr Darcy scrambling up the next fence, white glove still tucked firmly into his collar.

'Oh sherbet!' Dad squealed, going for the cat. 'We've got to grab him before he does any more damage. But whatever you do, Jim, don't touch the glove!' he called. 'You hold him still and I'll get it.'

'What about you?' I called behind. 'What if you touch it? You haven't got your black glove on –'

Dad stopped momentarily and turned around. I'd said too much.

'Black glove on the floor in your office,' I stammered. 'I'm guessing you use it for putting the white one on . . . so you don't die.' I gulped.

'I'll use my jumper sleeve . . .' He paused and I waited for accusations. But Dad's face relaxed. 'I'm proud of you, Jim. You'd make a good detective. That was the quickest bit of thinking since Mr Bean chopped his teddy in two to fit his suitcase.'

He'd lost me there. And I didn't want him to be proud of me. Not after what I'd done. But I couldn't wallow. We were in the middle of an emergency. Dad was turning in circles, calling 'kitty kitty' in a slightly strangled, uninviting way that no cat in its right mind would stop for. I peered over the fence on the other side of Mrs Dewsbury's garden.

In the next garden, I saw Mr Bagshot perched on a little rusty stool tending to his upside down bicycle, spinning the wheels round and round. And then I saw Mr Darcy making his approach.

'Why, hello there, Mr Darcy,' Mr Bagshot cooed.

I motioned to Dad and the two of us scrambled over the fence and landed with a double thump in Mr Bagshot's back garden. It startled him, but not Mr Darcy, who was making a feline beeline right for him.

'What do you think you're doing, Mr Wimple? Can't you ring on the doorbell?'

'Don't touch the cat!' Dad rasped, desperately.

'Oh, not to worry. Mr Darcy's a regular visitor to our house –'

'What are you doing with that bike?' I interrupted, hoping to stop him from patting the cat. Distraction, see?

'Wheels have got a squeak and I can't locate the –'

'Can you show me what you're doing?' I said quickly. 'My bike squeaks like crazy.'

'Well, I could I suppose, although I'd like to . . . Hello, Mr Darcy.'

'Could you show me right now, please!' I pleaded. 'I really *am* keen to know more about bicycles . . .' I pinned Mr Bagshot with a big eager smile, while Dad darted around after Mr Darcy in the background.

'Alright, then, Jim,' Mr Bagshot said, obviously won over by my enthusiasm. 'What you need is a can of WD40 oil. A bicycle is like any other machine, see?'

Mr Bagshot squirted the oil on to the wheel and spun it again. It whirred and purred beautifully . . . which probably wasn't the best outcome, as the noise well and truly attracted Mr Darcy, who sped towards the sound.

Before I could stop him, he leapt onto Mr Bagshot's shoulder, where he gently brushed the skin of his neck with the white glove.

Dad clutched his head, jumped up and down and shouted something rude at the sky. I gulped and looked at our neighbour, who had slumped back down onto his stool and then toppled backwards, legs in the air, dead as a dodo.

It didn't seem right to leave him there like that, looking so undignified. But we couldn't hang around. It was time for a Snappy Meal. I repeat: time for a Snappy Meal. Mr Darcy had already made his way through the back door of Mr Bagshot's house.

'We've got to get him before anyone else dies,' Dad shouted.

We ran into the house, where we found Mrs Bagshot, Darcy's latest victim. She had clearly been in the middle of doing the dishes when she patted the cat. If only she'd been wearing washing-up gloves she'd have been all right. But Dad and I both sobbed with despair at the sight of her lying on the floor, under a blanket of soapy bubbles. The cat was on the table, tucking into some leftovers on a plate. Dad let out a groan. The cat looked up and hissed, like he knew he was in trouble, and leapt from one piece of furniture to another, before darting further into the house and up the stairs. It's exactly what I'd do if I were being followed by a couple of sweaty, crazy-eyed people, yelling and running like it was the end of the world. But I didn't have time to feel sorry for Mr Darcy. We needed that glove. We followed him, puffing like steam trains, and checked all the rooms.

I was momentarily distracted by the enormous electric train set Mr Bagshot had in his spare room and briefly wondered, considering we lived so close, why he had never invited me over to see it.

'He's here!' I heard Dad call.

Mr Darcy was sitting on the window sill of the Bagshots' bedroom, in front of an open window. His green eyes looked at us, unimpressed, like we were fools wasting his time; his tail was flicking slightly. He was doing what cats do, but in my mind he'd become a master of cunning, a kitty of cruelty . . . I could see by the look on Dad's face, he felt the same.

Dad edged closer.

Mr Darcy remained very still.

'You can do it, Dad!' I whispered, and Mr Darcy turned his head slowly to me as if to sneer *oh really?*

Dad crept closer. He was an arm's-reach away. Closer. Closer. And then Mr Darcy elegantly leapt from the second-floor window to the street below, landing lightly on his soft paws and stopping to lick his bottom before toying with an ivy branch swaying in the wind.

'I've got an idea,' I said.

We left the way we came, through the back door and over the fence, leaving behind us Mr and Mrs Bagshot, who looked as if they'd come to a terrible end at the hands of a madman rather than a painless and quick death at the paws of a glove-toting cat. I felt bad about that, and if there had been time I would have moved them – to the sofa, at least, rather than sprawled on the ground. But there wasn't a moment to lose.

'What's your plan, son?' Dad puffed as we ran back towards our house.

'No time to explain,' I panted. And there wasn't. A cat was on the loose and it was in danger of spreading death quicker than buttery disaster on hot toast. No time to chew the details. It was time for a Snappy Meal. I repeat: time for a Snappy Meal.

Chapter 10

Dad and I drove the car round to Mr and Mrs Bagshot's front door. Mr Darcy was no longer there. But we knew which direction he'd taken, because three doors down we saw Jenny Lipsy's roller-skated feet poking out through her garden gates, and nine doors down Harold McDougal was leaning heavily into the low stone wall of his front garden, as if he'd fallen into a deep sleep while pruning his hedge. Mr Darcy must have been parading along the stone walls, attracting the attention of innocent neighbours. Mr Darcy was lethal. Right now he was nowhere to be seen but we were going to catch the elusive cat, because we had a plan.

Dad's car was an estate, meaning the boot is connected to the inside of the car – not a separate compartment. I had raided Hetty's room and found unidentified furry toys that we tied to strings and attached to the tow bar at the back of the car, along with household things like sponges and plugs on chains: things that would bounce and rattle as we drove up the street. We left the boot door open, and inside we placed comfy cushions and bowls of tinned tuna. With a plank of wood we made a ramp from the boot to the road below and attached a bag of cat treats to the top, sticky-taped at an angle that wouldn't let the treats pour out, but would let one or two loose every time the car jolted. The treats would roll down the ramp and create a tantalising treasure trail. The whole idea was to lure Mr Darcy, to coax him into the luxurious boot with the smell of tuna chunks, where he might make himself comfortable – and instantly trappable.

We drove slowly down the road, the rattle and squeak of toys bouncing behind us. Dad stuck his head out of the window. 'Mr Dar-cy . . . Mr *Dar-cy*,' he called over and over again in a flat voice. I was the lookout. I strained my eyes and my neck as I twisted left and right, back then front, trying to spot the elusive death cat.

There was no Mr Darcy.

After a while I turned round to check the boot, in case he'd climbed in without us noticing. There *was* a cat there – but it was a dirty tabby with one eye. He was happily nestling into one of the cushions.

'It's working. And I think we've attracted another cat,' I said, spying a scraggy newcomer. 'Next time it'll be Mr Darcy, Dad.'

In the boot was a brutish ginger, now fighting the one-eyed tabby for the cushion. While I was watching, a slinky grey Burmese and a black and white cat with a diamond collar jumped aboard. They began to nibble delicately at the tuna.

'Where is he?' Dad growled, through gritted teeth.

In the side mirror I could see even more cats that weren't Mr Darcy. In fact, there was a whole gang of cats catching up with us, attracted by the smells and squeaks and bounces of our modified Catmobile. One clung to a toy on a string like he was hitching a ride on a kite, and another began mounting the plank.

'Dad! I think we're attracting all the cats in the neighbourhood!'

'We can't stop,' Dad said. 'We need to find Mr Darcy before he wipes out the entire town . . . FLUMPETS!' he shouted, and I was scared then. I didn't know what *flumpets* meant, but

Dad's voice wasn't playful. I realised we were all in real trouble. Indigo, the Bagshots, Jenny Lipsy, Harold . . . How many more were there now?

Suddenly my tummy rumbled.

'What was that?' Dad said.

'My tummy. Haven't eaten since this morning. And all I had was one of Mum's health shakes.'

'Oh Lord, you poor thing,' said Dad, with real compassion. 'Have a look in the car-door pocket. There may be something. Should be a flapjack.'

Parking tickets, a book called *New Accountancy Laws* (a prop for his role as an accountant), a packet of flapjack crumbs and a bag of boiled sweets. I picked up the boiled sweets and stuffed one into my mouth.

I love the way boiled sweets look so boring – no sour sugar-tingles or chewy pieces –

but once you start sucking them they fill your mouth with juice. Will says the juice is actually a burst of your own saliva, which sounds disgusting but weirdly is the total opposite of disgusting. The one I had was raspberry flavour and it was like an explosion of the biggest sweetest fruit.

'Urgh. Can you stop making that noise, Jim, I'm trying to concentrate.'

'What noise?'

'That awful slurping!'

Slurping? It was precisely because of Will's revolting saliva-symphony that Mr Darcy turned up in the first place!

I stuck my head out of the window and began slurping loudly. Dad looked even more disgusted but there was no time to explain. I slurped and slurped and slurped. And then, in front of us, emerging from a garden, was Mr Darcy. I was running out of slurp but I forced the saliva back and forth over my tongue. My mouth was drying. SLURP!

Mr Darcy meandered towards us like a king strolling out of his castle to address his people. Dad slowed the car, the toys still rattling and twitching on the road behind us.

'Come on, Mr Darcy,' Dad and I pray-whispered together. 'Come on!'

He was behind the car now, facing the open boot. We both strained to look through the rear-view mirror. Mr Darcy was just about to put a front paw on the ramp – just two seconds away from being trapped. That's it, Mr Darcy. That's it! Nearly, then –

There was a screech behind us. Some lunatic braking hard on their bicycle. Mr Darcy ran back into the garden and out of sight. I could have killed that cyclist!

'There you are!' said Fiona, riding her bike level to the passenger window.

She looked amazing. Her untied black hair was wild from cycling fast, her wrists were wrapped with leather bands like a gladiator, her T-shirt had the words *Gruesome & Awesome* on it, her huge eyes were full of excitement. Excitement to see *me*!

But I couldn't let myself get distracted. Dad was making a strange, strangled noise in the seat next to me.

'Fiona, now isn't the time.'

'Please, Jim. Just a few minutes. I need you to show me the One-Touch . . .'

Dad had started to bang his forehead gently on the steering wheel. I had to end this now.

'Fiona. You need to go.'

'But, Jim!' she pouted.

'No!' I wound up the window.

I looked in the side mirror as we drove away. Fiona was straddling her bike, arms folded over her chest, head cocked to the side. I felt bad for her. I felt really bad for me. But I was pretty sure I hadn't heard the last of Fiona. She was more determined than a buffalo when she wanted to be. Not that she looked like a buffalo. Not at all. More like a deer with a . . . oh, never mind.

'That girl!' Dad growled.

'Yeah. That girl . . .' I replied, shaking my head.

Chapter 11

As much as I'd liked seeing Fiona, she had made things a lot worse. She'd blown our chance to catch Mr Darcy and now he had disappeared again. It'd take more than boiled sweets to catch him now.

Dad and I drove around the neighbourhood for ages looking for him, half out of our minds. We were a tiny bit relieved that the people we were passing in the street seemed to be upright and generally in good health. But when the sun started going down, we were hit with a new wave of panic.

Evening meant no light to find Mr Darcy. It also meant Mum and Hetty getting home, Mr Sinister losing his patience and Mum's yoga teacher wondering what had happened to his daughter. Dad and I wracked our brains for ideas but we had nothing but a handful of sweet wrappers and a boot full of cats. We needed manpower and womanpower – any power would do. We just needed help.

And I knew one person I definitely wanted on my team.

I didn't really want to get Will involved again but sometimes Will is just the person you need. When you listen to him talk, it's easy to think his brain is fuddled or muddled. But, actually, Will's brain is fresh. It's like he was born yesterday, in a good way. Think about it – if you had a brand new brain that wasn't bogged down with all the old habits and things you already know and think about over and over, it would probably come up with 'fresh' ideas. Get it? Well, trust me. I have sat through Will's lengthy nonsense explanations, and every now and then an idea pops out that makes you go, *Wow, why didn't I think of that?* Why, because I definitely don't have a Will-shaped brain.

I told Dad my idea. He couldn't deny that we needed more hands and more help, and we didn't need to explain the real reason to anyone. We could say that a neighbour was desperately worried about her missing cat, and we were the search party. Of course, it would also be better if we split up, went separate ways. And it was probably a good idea that Will didn't see Dad, who looked way too worried for a simple case of a missing pet, not to mention him having a boot full of random cats that refused to budge.

Dad dropped me outside Will's house. I gave him one of my walkie-talkies and said we'd be in touch. Will was standing in the doorway, watching me, looking mildly amused.

'Will, I need you for a mission,' I said, placing my hand firmly on his shoulder.

'You're taking this spy game very seriously, Jim,' he said, pointing to my walkie-talkie.

'It's not a game,' I said seriously.

'It's not?'

'We're after a ninja death cat, stalking the neighbourhood, spreading terror –' I stopped when I saw Will's eyes fill like paddling pools and his lip quiver. 'Not really, Will. We're looking for Mr Darcy.'

'That snail-tormenting cat with the fishhook claws?'

'The very same one. We need as many people to help as possible.'

From out of the corner of my eye I saw Dad drive away slowly. His face looked slightly crazed, as if he was being attacked by bees. Not surprising, really . . . This was death out of control, and he thought it was his fault. I felt really bad. Worse than I'd ever felt before. I had to make it right. I had to get that cat.

'We could ask Fiona to help too,' Will said. 'Come in for a minute.'

There wasn't much time for hanging around, but Will had disappeared back inside so I didn't have any choice. Besides, I love going to Will's house. His mum is hilarious and nice and kind. She's crazy about pop music and she's always dancing. Will and Fiona find it embarrassing, but I think it's fun. She also feeds me well. By that, I mean normal food.

Not stuff with nuts, seeds and grass in it.

When I stepped inside I was fully expecting to hear the usual clatter of pots and pans and Will's mum's bangles as she did the dishes while dancing to 'Shake Your Body Down'. But I didn't hear funk, hip-hop, pop or anything like that. The music that was flooding the house was . . . *opera*! What was going on?

Will's mum was standing in the middle of the kitchen, arms in the air, swaying like an opera diva. And she was covered in flour. She stopped when she saw me and grinned.

'All right, Jim Wimple, love?' She always calls me by my full name.

'Hi, Mrs Maggot. That's interesting music.'

'Oh, you haven't heard anything yet!' She flashed me an excited look, darted over to the stereo and turned up the volume. 'You just wait. One, two, three . . .'

A sudden heavy base beat joined the opera music. *Boom-boom-tra-la-laaaa!*

'I call it OpeRock!' she squealed. 'I mixed it, myself.'

Then Will's mum started head-banging and ballet twirling at the same time. The music sounded quite cool, like something off a really arty car advert. Will and I stood, both kind of mesmerised by his mum. I'm not sure it was in a good way. When she ran out of puff she opened the oven. 'Fancy some pizza, Jim Wimple, love?' She knows I love pizza. My tummy rumbled.

Mrs Maggot pulled out a pizza. But it wasn't the heavily cheesed frozen pizzas she normally got out of a packet. It was thin, ultra-crispy, and it wasn't exactly round, either. It had wobbly edges and thick tomato sauce flecked with herbs.

'I made it!' she cried. 'From scratch! *Italiano,
doncha-know*. Here, have a slice.'

She didn't have to ask me twice. It was piping
hot but absolutely delicious. Because of Mum's
experimental cooking, I've always been
suspicious when parents try to make ordinary

foods in a special way. Like Mum's McChickpea Burger. But this was amazing. Better than any pizza I'd tried before – crispy and light, but deeply tomatoey with puddles of mozzarella and pepperoni.

'She's been doing an Italian cookery class,' Will told me. 'Our fridge is full of delicatessen food. It's driving me a bit crazy, to be honest.'

Fiona stomped into the kitchen, scowling at the music, but she softened when she saw me. 'Hi, Jim.' She smiled. She looked at me expectantly, as if she thought I was here just for her.

'Hi, Fiona. I've actually come round to ask for people to help us search for a missing cat.'

'Oh.'

'Will's coming.' I turned around but Will had gone. 'Er . . .'

'I've actually got my karate lesson in ten minutes. Can't miss a lesson. I'm extremely dedicated to it. My sensei says that with my determination I can get to black belt in no time. Black belt,' she said again, triumphantly.

I didn't doubt it.

'But see you later?' she added hopefully. She skipped out of the door, which was very unlike Fiona. Fiona usually slinked and prowled like a nonchalant tiger.

'If I didn't know better, I'd think she was trying to impress you, Jim Wimple,' Will's mum winked.

I didn't know what to say to that. But I had to get Will. We had to get on our way. Dad was out there alone, worried, scared. And here I was eating pizza, enjoying some unusually nice attention and acting as if it was a normal Saturday in a normal person's life. And my life just isn't normal. Today of all days illustrated that.

The fear set in.

I was shaking slightly as I ran up to Will's bedroom.

'Will, come on!' I panted.

'Oh, hi, Jim,' he said, holding out his arms. He was wearing his Will-Magico outfit, but I noticed that to one arm he'd taped lettuce leaves and to the other, cucumber slices.

'What are you doing?' I said, taking a step forward.

'Stop!' he cried, so loudly that I jumped backwards. He motioned with his eyes to the floor in front of my feet, where Maximus, his pet giant African land snail, was unfurling.

'What are you *doing*?' I cried. This really was no time to start games with one of the slowest creatures on Earth.

'Snails can smell their favourite foods from metres away – their sense of smell is brilliant.

So you've entered at the start of a very exciting experiment. I'm seeing if a) he can smell the food, and b) if he can tell me which food is his favourite.'

For Will, this is education and entertainment rolled into one perfect package, and any other time I'd have been happy to join in, being his best friend and everything, but NOT NOW!

'Will. You're supposed to be helping me. The cat, remember?'

'Oh yes. Sorry, Jim,' Will said, ripping the vegetation off his arms and popping it into Maximus's tank. He plucked the snail off the floor and put him there too.

'We're running out of time –'

'Why?'

'Because Mr Darcy goes to bed at eight.' *What was I saying?* 'We need to act fast. What do you know about cats?'

'Nothing. But I know a lot about molluscs.' Will didn't really need to tell me this. I sighed heavily and he tutted at my lack of enthusiasm. 'The whole world is connected, Jim. The whole world is connected.'

It was one of Will's favourite phrases, and actually, he had managed to prove it was true on a couple of occasions. But I wasn't so sure this time, and we didn't have time to lose.

'There is no way catching a cat is in any way connected to the mollusc family,' I said firmly.

'It depends where you make the connections, Jim,' he replied, pulling on his magician's cape. 'You'll see.'

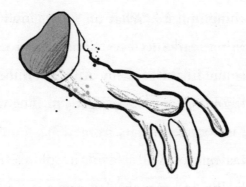

Chapter 12

We were now armed with everything we might need that was related to molluscs and, in a strange way, also to cats. I knew he could do it. I knew he could connect them somehow. Will had packed everything in a backpack the size of Belgium, which included:

1. A torch.
   Will said, some squid glow in the dark to lure food, find a mate and

communicate. What on a cat glows in the dark? Its eyes, so long as you shine a light at them. And when they light up, they really light up! Bingo!

2. Delicatessen meats from Will's mum's fridge.

Will said, although he hadn't completed his own personal experiment with Maximus, it was common knowledge that snails had a great sense of smell and went for their favourite foods. Cats, too, would not be able to resist the tastiest of treats. The food had to be good. *Really* good. *Italiano* good.

3. Night-vision goggles.

'Octopuses are masters of disguise,' Will explained. 'They can change colour to hide against the background.

I'm thinking, in the case of a cat, who can't change colour, it would choose to change background instead. A black cat wouldn't stand in front of a white wall if it wanted to hide, would it? It would hide in the darkness. So I've also packed night-vision goggles.'

Most of these were pretty flimsy mollusc–cat connections, but Will said that although a length of string was floppier than a steel pole, it had just as many uses. And I couldn't argue with that.

'I didn't know you had night-vision goggles.'

'Dad bought them when he thought we had mice. He stayed up all night trying to catch sight of one. He gave up and gave them to me, so I could watch what Maximus does at night without turning my lights on. You should try it.'

I knew he was dying to tell me more about Maximus's night-time behaviours, but we had to go. We popped into the kitchen to say goodbye to Will's mum, who was listening to a Mozart/Lady GaGa mash-up and kneading more pizza dough. It had fennel seeds in it, she said. I wondered for a moment if she and my mum might have more in common than I had first thought.

'Have fun, boys!' She waved at us with a floury hand. Her bangles were caked together. 'Oh, and, Jim Wimple, love – Fiona's set off for her karate lesson, but she says to let you know that she'll come and find you later.'

The thought of Fiona eager to find me later filled my heart with both excitement and fear – like a trout fisherman who's finally got a catch, only to reel in a colossal squid.

There was a crackle. Dad on the walkie-talkie!

'Yes, Dad?' I said, walking outside so our conversation was private.

'*You need to get home! I saw Mum's car – she's on her way back with Hetty from shopping. If she sees Indigo . . .*'

'I'll go right away.'

'*Just explain everything to Mum. Stop Hetty from going in the garden.*'

'Okay,' I croaked. Mum knows about Dad, obviously, but it's not something we talk about. And I wasn't sure I could keep calm. I had to, of course. I had to be the strong one. Dad was falling to pieces. 'Any luck finding Mr Darcy, Dad?'

The crackling ended. I guessed there was no luck.

I explained to Will that I needed to pop home and deliver a message.

'What about Mr Darcy's bedtime?' Will said,

shaking his head. 'Because at this rate, he'll be losing snooze time.'

At home, Mum and Hetty were already back from shopping, and Mum was whizzing up something horrible in a blender. Hetty was examining some chocolate biscuit crumbs she'd found on the kitchen table. I ran in and said hello in an over-the-top kind of way.

'What's wrong, darling?' Mum said, looking at my grim expression, which must have been similar to the one I wear when she gives me health food. 'Don't worry about this – it looks strange, but it's actually a Wheatgrass Super Smoothie. Hetty said we should call it a Wheatgrass Wooper-Smoothie.'

'Actually, I said Pooper-Woobie,' Hetty said.

But I wasn't worried about Mum's health food or what it was called. Not at all.

'You haven't been in the garden, either of you?' I said. I tried to sound casual. But it come out as casual as a police officer with constipation. Mum shook her head and looked at me funny. She sensed something was up.

'Will, can you chat to Hetty while I have a word with Mum?'

I took Mum into the living room and told her everything. Well, not everything. Everything I could without landing myself in deep trouble. After dropping her glass of Pooper-Woobie Smoothie on the floor, Mum nodded and gathered me in her arms. She said that we were a team, and we should treat this as a test to see how strong our teamwork was. Sometimes Mum's life-explanations are annoying, but I found this one quite comforting, and I hugged her back.

We discussed the hunt for Mr Darcy and how

she and Hetty could help. Hetty obviously couldn't know the full story – she wasn't ready to cope with that kind of information. Not because she's too sweet and innocent. Quite the opposite. Hetty is great at finding out secrets, but not so good at keeping them. She'd sell anything for her horse fund. But she had to be involved somehow because she couldn't stay in the house on her own, and she couldn't be allowed to venture out into the garden . . .

Mum and I went back to Will and Hetty in the kitchen.

'Jim, would you rather fall to your death from a cliff or be buried alive?' Will asked me.

'Not you, too, Will,' I moaned. 'Come on, let's look for that cat.'

'Only if you answer Will's question,' said Hetty.

'Okay. Buried alive.'

'Wrong answer,' Will said. 'Being buried alive is a very frightening death.'

'So is falling off a cliff.'

'Yes, but at least you have scenery. Distraction – see?' Will high-fived Hetty.

'Nothing is straightforward, Jimble Wimble,' Hetty said, wagging a finger.

No. Nothing at all was straightforward today.

Would you rather kill a snail by crushing it and suffer lengthy guilt, or try to do it nicely and end up chasing a killer cat around the neighbourhood?

Chapter 13

We were all set to go.

Mum and Hetty were going to knock on doors and talk to neighbours. They would give out Mum's mobile phone number as a Cat Hotline for anyone who spotted Mr Darcy. We called Dad and found out where he was, and then we scattered to different parts of the neighbourhood. Dad had the car, Mum and Hetty took the grown-up bike and trailer, and Will and I hopped back on our bikes, armed with a torch, fine-cut salami and night-vision goggles.

We searched high and low for Mr Darcy but with every minute that passed it was looking more and more desperate. Every black cat we came across had a white patch of some sort – a paw, ear or tummy – but not a glove. Will was trying his best to be upbeat, but he was flagging. His legs were starting to tire and his random conversation petered out.

Things were getting so miserable I stopped walkie-talkie-ing Dad after a while; every time I did he sounded more and more despairing, like a lost child, and my eyes kept filling up with tears, which made it hard to see. I wanted my next call to Dad to be positive. But nothing could get rid of the bitter feeling I had in my stomach – that bitter feeling of being a fraud. He thought I was his super-son, trustworthy and true. But I wasn't super or trustworthy. I was a kid who put curiosity first and let the cat out of the bag. I was bad.

I pushed on, bribing Will with a promise to help him the next day with his Anti-Escargot Campaign. And help him write his blog on freshwater bivalves (that's river mussels to you and me).

We cycled round and round for another hour, searching the shadows, stopping to look behind every wall and shrubbery in every front garden. Then, finally, a crackle came through on the walkie-talkie.

'Dad?'

'*Someone phoned Hetty on the Cat Hotline. Mr Darcy was spotted in the high street.*'

'Brilliant! We'll head straight over.'

'*We'll close ranks behind you.*'

'It'll be okay, Dad.'

I could almost hear him smile a little. Not a lot. But I could sense a twitch of hope.

We had known Mr Darcy wouldn't roam out of town – he wasn't that fast, and besides, he had comfy sofas and food available at nearly every house in the neighbourhood, so why would he bother? But knowing the search area had been narrowed to the high street was encouraging. The high street was brightly lit even at night, with only doorways to hide in. There were odd alleys in between shops, which led to dumpsters and parallel streets, but at least we had a chance.

Will and I set off at super-speed with new enthusiasm. When we got there, we rode up and down the deserted street, our eyes peeled for a cat. We didn't see a living thing except for Wizard Bob, who is a locally famous homeless man who wears a pointy hat, mumbles like he's recanting spells and sleeps in the doorway of Quids-In discount store. He was leaning heavily against the bolted doors, his mouth open. I motioned for Will to stop, and I jumped off my bike and ran to see if he had made the mistake of stroking a proud black cat with a deadly accessory. I peered closely into Wizard Bob's still face.

He jumped like an electrocuted frog when he opened his eyes and saw me looking at him. I jumped too. And then Will squealed, because we were all a bit jumpy. Wizard Bob started gathering his things around him protectively.

'Hi, Wizard Bob,' I said. 'I didn't mean to disturb you. I just wondered if you'd seen a black cat walk down here in the last fifteen minutes.'

'Yes. Cat. Catkins in a butter dish, spreading all the fleas. Cat. Yes, cat.'

'Could you tell me which way it went?'

'This way that way, took my sausage roll,' Wizard Bob muttered. 'He nickleby nicked it! T'was here, now gone. Cat thief. Beware the naughty whiskers . . .'

'Oh dear. Sorry about your sausage roll.'

'Hungry, I am. Hungry, I will be. For a cat did come and pinch my tea.'

Wizard Bob started sobbing gently. We couldn't leave him like that! I looked at Will, who shrugged back at me. I took the rucksack and retrieved the bag of delicatessen meats, intended for luring the cat.

'Here . . .' I popped the little bag at Wizard Bob's feet. 'Which way did naughty whiskers go?'

'Tuppenny Lane.'

'Excellent. Thanks, Wizard Bob.'

'Call me Wizard Bob.'

'He just did,' Will said, but I did a lip-zip

motion. Sometimes there was no point in trying to understand why Wizard Bob said the things he did. Sometimes he and Will had a lot in common.

'Any use, Jim?' Will said.

'Yes. He's given us a lead.' I looked at Will, who was looking confused. 'Not a dog lead, Will. A lead. A *clue*!'

'*Jim, anything?*'

It was Dad on the walkie-talkie radio. 'Hi, Dad. We've got a lead. He's gone down Tuppenny Lane. I'll call you when we see him.'

'*Oh that's great news, Jim. Go get him! But be careful. Don't touch him.*'

'It's okay. I remember.'

I looked at Will, who was still looking confused. 'Fleas. Can't touch him.'

'That's going to be tricky,' Will said, rolling his eyes. And that was the next most sensible thing he'd said since the last sensible thing he said. Two in a day!

Tuppenny Lane was a little passageway – a cut-through for people shopping on the high street who wanted to go to the supermarket. There was no lighting here. We needed our torches. Halfway down Tuppenny Lane we came across a lady on a bench, shopping bag at her side. She easily looked as if she could be asleep, but not only was it past closing time, there was something in her angle – she was tilted slightly sideways – and I knew the cat had struck again. I touched her cheek and it was hot. A recent kill by the innocent but deadly dangerous Mr Darcy. I told Will she was meditating. He said it looked as if I had just given her the One-Touch.

So Mr Darcy had definitely gone down Tuppenny Lane. Next stop, Pluckers the

Supermarket. At this time of night the car park was always crawling with cats, who turned up to see what out-of-date foods had been thrown out. I know that, because Mum once remarked on it – she'd gone down to the bins to see if she could salvage some of the fruit and veg that 'had plenty of life left in it'.

We approached the back of Pluckers and it was pitch black. Will raised his torch and swept it over the wide, empty, tarmac space towards the rows of giant bins. Dozens of eyes lit up like luminous marbles. Cats! There were cats everywhere. The place was writhing with them. As we got closer we could make out their shapes and then their colours. None of them ran – they just looked at us as if we were very rude to interrupt their midnight feast. And then, perched on top of a bin, with a paw in a pot of cream, we saw Mr Darcy.

'Look!' I whispered. 'There he is. But how are we going to get him?'

'This is a job for Will-Magico!' said Will. 'Let me consult my knowledge on animal magic tricks.' He was silent for a while. 'I've got it. I'm going to infiltrate the cat gang.'

'You're going to pretend to be a cat?'

'Yes, but we need to get closer.'

It sounded crazy, but Will's ideas were sometimes made of gold, and I didn't have any ideas of my own. None of us had thought about how to catch Mr Darcy without a car-boot trap.

We tiptoed closer and closer, Will first, me behind. Some of the cats bristled and looked ready to run. One of those cats was Mr Darcy. But still, we were getting nearer and so far none of them had. Maybe this *was* a job for Will-Magico! We were within a whisker of the cat gang. Some had already started to slink away, but not Mr Darcy. Will reached into his pocket and retrieved his noise machine. Before I could say a word, he pressed a button –

MMRRREEEOOOWWWW

Mr Darcy shot two feet in the air and then bolted.

'What the hell did you do that for?' I yelled.

'I was mimicking. It's a really efficient magic trick used by animals. I was just trying to make my cat infiltration more authentic –'

'That machine miaow could have meant anything. For all you know, it said "someone's let the dogs out".'

'Who let the dogs out?' Will asked.

'Never mind. We need to follow that cat! Come on!'

I took the lead, grabbed Will's mission-ready rucksack, jumped on my bike and cycled off in the direction Mr Darcy had escaped. Over the road and into the park. I turned behind me to see Will rummaging in the bins.

'What are you doing?' I shouted angrily.

'Some of this stuff is good enough to eat!' he exclaimed, ducking his head back inside a giant wheelie bin.

'Are you going to help or not!' I called back. But I'd had enough. Will-Magico wasn't up to the challenge. His connections weren't making sense. His magic was non-existent. He was just making everything a lot worse. I had to go it alone. I cycled off without him.

I dumped my bike at the entrance to the park and walkie-talkied Dad to let him know where the cat chase was at. I didn't mention

Will's mimicry catastrophe, or the fact that I was out of salami and had no idea how to catch Mr Darcy single-handed, even if I did see him . . . But I made it sound as if I was in control.

It was hard as I really wasn't – the park was very, very dark, and kind of spooky. It had a playground with swings and roundabouts that squeaked and moaned like broken violins as they turned in the breeze. Heart thumping, I flashed the torch left, right, in front and behind. Wherever I shone the light, little creatures scuttled for the shadows. Perhaps Mr Darcy, too, would be avoiding the light. That cat, no matter how tricky, was probably more petrified than I was, after being chased by sweet-slurping, fake-miaowing maniacs. He'd have to be crazy to give himself up. If he had any sense, he'd melt into the shadows too.

Bingo!

Will had got one thing right. The night-vision goggles!

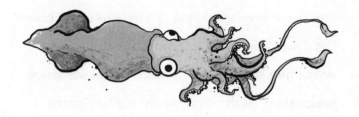

Chapter 14

Everything looks green through night-vision goggles. I swept my gaze around the park as I walked hesitantly forward, picking up green squirrels, green bugs, green mice. And a green cat.

There he was. Mr Darcy.

He was sitting under a bench, curled into a ball, tail flicking, scared eyes like green saucers. The bright white glove was a little stained by its trip to the rubbish bins, but it was still safely under his collar – phew! This was my chance – perhaps my *last* chance. I HAD to catch him. But I was alone. In a T-shirt. With no way of protecting my hands. I looked at the rucksack and, as if Will were with me, thought of molluscs . . . In particular, a giant clam!

With the zip undone, I approached Mr Darcy with the open rucksack, using my slurping noise and a couple of miaow sounds I hoped wouldn't mean 'someone's let some more dogs out' or anything alarming. He sat and watched as I crept closer. Closer and closer. Success was just a paw's-length away. I opened the bag wider, ready to engulf the cat and zip it up tight. So very nearly there –

CLUNK

I hit my head on the bench seat and yelped. Mr Darcy leapt over my body and ran back towards the park entrance.

I could have said something really rude, but I was too upset even to shout 'FLUMPETS'. My brain was hurting, my head was hurting, and I knew that I had hurt many people in my failure to just come clean and tell the truth.

Sobbing, I limped back up the path towards my bike. But I stopped abruptly.

Through my night-vision goggles I saw a green shape on the floor up ahead. A body. It had arms and legs spread like a starfish and a black piece of cloth spread over the torso. I held my breath. Was it a dead body? A collapsed body? Whose body *was* it?

I froze as I saw Mr Darcy circle the body, then leap up on to the cloth-covered chest. The cat sniffed the cloth and then licked. Licked again. He was eating something! I could still get him – all was not lost!

I crept closer, swallowing my fear of the anonymous body. As I did so, I saw that the cloth was scattered with flecks of food and Mr Darcy was lapping them up. He was so distracted by the grub that he wasn't watching me. I could grab him. I could get him right now. But if I did, it would have to be with my hands, and I might die. I gulped and stepped forward. It was the only way to stop this. The only way. I would have to be brave, and embrace death if that's what it took . . .

I counted: one, two, thr—

'Gotcha!'

The body's arms contracted suddenly and folded the cape inwards, trapping Mr Darcy.

I ripped off the night-vision goggles and shone my torch at Will, who was sitting upright with a wriggling package on his lap, grinning from ear to ear.

'That move is what botanists would call the Venus flytrap, although I like to think of my move as more of an angler fish. They lure their prey right into their jaws.'

I laughed. 'I don't care what trick it is, Will-Magico. It's brilliant!'

'All thanks to the bins at Pluckers,' he smiled, brushing some fish flakes from his cape.

CRACKLE

'*Any luck, Jim?*'

'Yes, Dad. We got him. We got him!' I was crying with relief and happiness. Dad whooped.

'*Terrific, Jim. I'm parked just outside the park. Where are you?*'

'Just inside the park, Dad. We'll be there in a jiffy.'

We ran towards Dad's car and I opened the boot. Will lowered his arms and opened his cape. Mr Darcy leapt into the car, coming nose to nose with a bunch of cats.

'Is he in?' Dad called from the front.

I walked around to his window and smiled. 'Yes, he's in, Dad.' I noticed Dad's face looked older than usual. The stress he'd been under . . . He managed a bold smile. I gave him the thumbs up. Several times.

Dad leaned out of his window to give me the biggest hug. We turned around to look at the cat. Mr Darcy looked up and saw us watching, suspicious, tail curled around his feet.

'We got him!' I shouted again in glee and punched the air, ignoring the strange look I was getting from a woman walking her dogs on the pavement opposite. 'Let's get the cat home!'

Dad drove off, and I fell to my knees in exhaustion.

'I hope whoever owns that cat is extremely grateful,' Will said, putting his hand on my shoulder. 'Because you have put your heart and soul into this.'

'And so have you, Will.' I smiled. 'I couldn't have done it without you.'

'You don't mean that,' Will said shyly.

'I do, you know. You were magic.'

We rode home in an exhausted silence, thinking about how everything's connected – sometimes not in an obvious way, but a piece of flimsy string has as many uses as a steel pole. Actually, Will might not have been thinking about that at all. He could have been contemplating the strength of a human bicep compared with the force of a closing giant clam, or whether it's possible to invent a sign language using facial expressions. You never could tell.

But he was grinning ear to ear, his magician's cape flapping in the wind. And that was good enough for me.

Chapter 15

When we got home, it looked as if Dad had parked at speed. The car was diagonal across the driveway. I dropped my bike and while Will was untangling his cape from his handlebars, I quickly peered in at all the cats in the back, sleeping, circling, slapping each other with big puffy paws. Mr Darcy was sitting very still, his green eyes cold and glaring. Definitely moody.

Dad came out. He wasn't looking happy

either, but colour had come back to his cheeks. He looked less deathly, at least.

'You've been a great help tonight, Will,' he said. 'Why don't you go inside and get something to drink.' Will shrugged, dropped his bike and went in. Dad turned to me.

'Jim, we need to get that cat inside. We need to secure the glove. It's time to extract Mr Darcy. I just want you to hold this blanket. If the cat somehow darts around me, throw the blanket on him and grab him, quick. We are not letting him get away.'

Dad decided to go in through the front – if we opened the boot, then all manner of cat hell could break loose. I stood by the driver's door with the blanket held out, while Dad scrambled over the driver's seat to the back passenger seat and then over the back passenger seat and into the boot, where he grabbed Mr Darcy to a chorus of miaows. I noticed he was wearing ski gloves.

'Gotcha!' he cackled as the cat bristled and let out an almighty miaow. I'm pretty sure it was a cat swear word worse than anything on Will's sound machine.

Dad backed out carefully, holding the angry cat tight to his chest. The glove was tight under his collar. Finally, we had everything under control.

We rushed inside with our furry prize and ran straight to the study, where we shut the door and locked it. When the glove was safely back in its box and Mr Darcy had been dispatched through the window and into the garden, we high-fived and laughed and high-fived some more and laughed again. Then Dad turned to me.

'Thank you, Jim,' he said, with tears in his eyes.

'What for?'

'I couldn't have done it without you.'

Well, without me you wouldn't have had to do it in the first place . . .

'That's not true,' I gulped.

'Yes is it, son. You're the one who had the great ideas – the Catmobile and all the cat-catching tricks. And not to mention the boiled sweets! Who knew that cats liked slurping noises!'

I blushed, and secretly thanked Will. My mate really was the best friend.

'Why don't you relax while I try to put things straight?' he said and ruffled my hair.

I looked at my Dad and soaked in all the kindness that I didn't deserve. 'Wait, Dad,' I said. I took a big breath. 'I think it's *me* that needs to put some things straight. The glove, the cat, the total sticky mess – it was all because of –'

Dad put his fingers to my lips. 'I think I've

worked it all out, Jim. It doesn't matter how wiggly the road was, so long as you get to the right destination. No point in complicating things now, eh?'

Dad winked and left me to wonder how much he knew, and if what he thought he knew was the same as what I knew. Unless we lay our cards on the table, this situation had no chance of being properly straightened out. I would show him my hand later. As soon as he'd finished his call.

While Dad was on the phone to The Dead End Office I walked slowly back towards the kitchen. Mum, Hetty and Will were discussing the Great Cat Chase. I caught Mum's eye and she winked at me and put her hand on her chest. It meant *what a relief*.

I felt almost delirious with relief myself, although it wasn't over. Outside the back door was Indigo. Down the road were more poor victims of the Great Cat Chase – the Bagshots, Mr McDougal, Jenny Lipsy . . . And down an alley leading to Pluckers the Supermarket was a lady slumbering on a bench by her shopping bag (I hoped she hadn't bought stuff that needed to go in the fridge). And while I was now free to recover from the chaos, Dad was still making sure that all these 'Mishaps' would be corrected.

Dad wouldn't like me listening in – and right now I never ever wanted to go against his wishes ever again – but I also couldn't just sit around. If Dad was going to be made to feel shame, then I needed to feel it too. I crept to the upstairs phone and lifted the receiver in time to hear the voice of Mr Sinister say:

'Well this is a fine mess. How many dead? Five . . . six? We don't even know for sure.

You've done this with your carelessness, Reaper. You left the glove in a vulnerable position, unsecured, unwatched, unlocked. And what happened? A cat got it. You were lucky a buffalo didn't get to it first – although with the chaos that cat's caused, it may as well have been a buffalo! It's going to be a major clean-up operation for Corrections and you know we can't keep calling in funds and favours to cover up for your mistakes. It uses up enormous resources to reverse a death. Enormous.'

Dad listened to Mr Sinister's lecture patiently, without saying a word. If that didn't make me feel bad enough, I knew that he hadn't yet found out about Mr Sinister's plans for his promotion to Misadventures, yet . . . That was going to be the biggest blow of all. This was so unfair.

When Dad came back downstairs he gave me a really big hug. He took my hand in his. Together we walked into the kitchen, where life had been frozen – Hetty, Mum and Will stilled in midconversation. The chatter had ceased, the kitchen clock had stopped ticking. I closed my hands tighter around Dad's. I had a notion that if I let go, then I'd be frozen too.

We walked into the garden. I noticed there was no breeze outside, no sound; the birds sat still in the trees. The only things moving were the two shadowy figures bent over Indigo.

'They're taking a long time, Dad. Do you think she'll be okay?'

'I don't know, really,' he said. 'I've never seen a Correction before.'

'I don't think I want to watch,' I said, with a lump in my throat. We turned to face the other way.

'Well, it was an adventure,' Dad said after a few moments. Now was the time.

'Dad, I need to tell you something.'

'No you don't,' Dad said softly. 'I think we've all learned some lessons today. And unless you're *curious* to know what lessons I'm talking about exactly, I think we should lay it to rest.'

I wasn't entirely sure what lessons he was talking about, but there was something about the way he said 'curious' . . .

'Shall we go out into the street and see the others?' I said, keen to see that everyone was all right.

To my surprise, he nodded. We walked back past the paused figures of Mum, Hetty and Will at the table – I noticed Hetty was holding a chocolate biscuit in her lap under the table. Her food crime, frozen in time.

Up and down our road dark characters were working their magic on the victims of Mr Darcy – or me, because, let's be honest, Mr Darcy never knew what he was doing. He was just going from house to house, gathering affection and food, like he always did. And the people were all happy to give it, like they always were. And I guess I was doing what I always do – looking for the nicest way to treat people and animals, including snails, and trying to put right mistakes I make. I never make them on purpose. It's always because of curiosity. Although I now know what it means when they say 'curiosity killed the cat'. Or a version of it, anyway. And Dad knows it too.

As the dark figures stood up, a wind started to play in the folds of their cloaks, and they began to run in a tight huddle away from the scene. They were wearing very nifty white trainers. I knew from previous encounters with the Death Department that they never skimped on trainers. Then birds began tweeting, traffic and household noises resumed. The Corrections Team was gone, and time was back.

The neighbours got to their feet and stood up straight and dusted themselves off as if they'd done nothing more than trip over a paving slab. I watched with a dropped jaw as Jenny Lipsy roller-skated out into the street and did a little twirl. She had no idea she'd died, or, as she waved at me, that it was me who killed her.

'What about people who might have seen them?' I asked.

'Seen what?' Dad said, with mock surprise. 'Nothing to see here. There never was.'

There would be no gossip at the tills in the supermarket or in the queues at the post office, no family wondering why Jenny had been out roller-skating for so long. It was just an ordinary day.

Dad squeezed my hand and let go. 'Promise you won't tell?' he said.

'I absolutely promise,' I said, and I meant it from the bottom of my heart.

Dad looked at me for a long time, and just when I thought he didn't believe me, he winked.

'Shall we go and see if Indigo is awake?' I said.

'Are you sure we'd be able to tell the difference,' Dad said with a nudge.

Chapter 16

When we got home Indigo was in the kitchen with the others and whatever conversation they were having was inaudible because of the noise of the blender.

Poor Indigo. I never thought I'd say that – she's really not my favourite person – but after today I knew I'd put up with her moods and her mobile phone and her total lack of interest in anything but her nails forever more.

'There you are,' Mum shouted over the noise. 'Where have you been?'

'I, er, nothing, sort of,' I stumbled. 'Hi, Indigo,' I said.

Mum stopped what she was doing, looked at Indigo and then at the ceiling, like she was thinking very hard. Then it must have dawned on her that time had passed and things had been made good again, because she looked back at me and Dad, breathed a deep sigh and smiled a big smile. She had some algae in her teeth, but I didn't mind. I ran and gave her a huge squeeze.

'Would you rather die by falling in a loo or by drinking goblin pee?' Hetty giggled. She was having a thumb war with Will, who was trying so hard his tongue was sticking out. He was losing. 'Where were you?' she said, looking up at me accusingly from under her wonky fringe.

'He was in the loo,' Mum interrupted.

'Oh good,' chipped in Will, wincing as he lost the thumb war to Hetty. 'Hope everything was okay. It's just that your mum thought that maybe you haven't been getting enough fibre in your diet lately.'

'Stop!' I shouted. 'Everyone, please! What I do in the loo is none of your business.'

'Your health is certainly *my* business, Jim.' Mum grinned. 'Here, drink this.'

She handed me the concoction. I held it up to the light, not that any light got through it. It looked more like a symptom than a cure. I looked at Dad pleadingly.

'Maybe later, darling,' Dad said. 'Jim's got a visitor.'

She appeared in the kitchen doorway, like a vision of Viking loveliness. She was wearing karate whites, her hair scraped back into two buns either side of her head, her cat-like eyes gleaming.

'Hi, Jim.'

'Hi, Fiona . . .'

Will sighed. 'I supposed you've come to take me home.'

'Yes, but first I want to spend some time with Jim,' she said, smiling. It was a smile so big her dimples almost turned into brackets.

There was only one reason she wanted to spend time with me, and I had to tell her the truth. I had to tell her that I didn't know the One-Touch at all. But Will had seen it with his own eyes. How was I going to get around that?

It was time for teamwork.

'Dad, can I have a quick word?'

We went into the study and I explained (without explaining too much) that Fiona had got it into her head that I was some kind of ninja master, and I wasn't, and I would lose face big time when I admitted that a snail had more ninja capabilities in its little finger than I had in my whole body. I also said that I thought Will might have worked out that the Great Cat Chase was more about life and death than a lost pet. It was another little lie, but this lie was for the best.

Dad said he knew what I was saying.

Fiona and Will had been memory-wiped before, when they got too close to Dad's truth, and even though I was terrified of having it done myself, I knew it didn't do any real harm – they were still my best friend and my best friend's awesome sister; they weren't lobotomised. One more time wouldn't hurt.

'Fiona, let's go outside,' I said. I wanted her to myself, just for one last moment.

Out in the garden, I stood with my hands in my pockets. Fiona approached me with a slow swagger, coming so close we were nose to nose and I could see deep into her incredible green eyes.

'Will told me what you did,' she said with a

sigh. 'And it was awesome. You,' she said, playfully poking me in the chest, 'are awesome.'

We stood looking at each other for a while. Fiona expectantly. Me, filled head to toe with thrills. But now she'd done all the sweet talk, she wanted me to give her the secret of the One-Touch. Time was up.

I looked up at Dad, who was at the back door waiting for my cue, as we planned. I gave him the thumbs up. He brought Will outside with him. Fiona was unfazed by their presence. She held my eye contact like a dedicated hypnotist.

'Did he show you how to do it?' Will said to Fiona.

'He's just about to, aren't you, Jim?' she said to me, trying to wave him away and not breaking eye contact for a second. I felt myself nod, although I didn't mean to.

Her eyes widened and melted into mine. She stood, waiting, looking at me like I was the most awesome example of awesomeness there ever was, and I let her.

'So you really think you're ready for the One-Touch?' I asked nervously.

She stared at me with extra awesomeness power, until I thought her eyes would explode with adoration. And when I thought I'd soaked enough of it in to remember forever, I reached out my hand to Dad.

Dad took it.

There was just a gentle breeze this time. It played through our hair and across the tips of the grass at our feet. Dad squeezed my hand tightly and looked down at my face, which I knew was glowing with embarrassment and pleasure all at once.

And just like that, the One-Touch was

forgotten. And so were all the good things that came with it.

A few moments later, free from adoration and all thoughts of my ninja mastery, Fiona was back to her Viking self, leaning against the wall of the hallway, telling us she was bored of waiting.

'What are we doing here anyway?' she snarled.

'Er . . .' Will scratched his head. 'I think Jim called us over.'

'Yes, Will. I just wanted to find out how Maximus's food experiment went, and to tempt you to watch an episode of *Spongebob*.'

'It's a bit late in the evening, Jim,' Will said.

'You're right. It is late. Perhaps tomorrow afternoon?'

'Yeah, all right. Although I'm a bit tired of *Spongebob*, actually.'

'You, bored of *Spongebob*?!'

'I know. I think I might be ready for something starring real people. I mean, actors are just pretending, aren't they? No one is actually in danger, or falling out of an aeroplane or getting attacked by aliens. It's just mimicry, isn't it? Really good mimicry. Nothing more.'

'I think you are definitely ready, Will.' I smiled.

'I'll miss Gary the Snail, though.'

'Not if you watch TV with Maximus in your lap. A real-life snail.'

'You're right, Jim,' he said, looking at me brightly. 'So tomorrow can I bring over a DVD of *Harry Potter* – the one where they turn back time?'

I cocked my head to one side and blinked. 'That one's my favourite, Will,' I said, and gave him a hug.

'Careful, Jim, your mum's only just put me in perfect alignment. You'll make me lose balance!'

Then the phone rang. I saw Dad tense. He walked upstairs.

'Will, you'd better go. See you tomorrow?'

'Righto!'

'Bye, Fiona.'

She looked at me with as much admiration as you'd look at bird poo on a pavement and left without saying a word.

After Dad disappeared upstairs, I sneaked to the downstairs phone and lifted the receiver.

'Well, the clean-up went pretty smoothly, and all in all, you've been very lucky. No one will remember a thing. I take it you haven't allowed anyone – and by anyone I mean ANYONE – to remember what happened here? . . . Good. We're not firing

you, because we like you, Reaper, we really do. Instead, as a punishment, we've decided not to give you the promotion you were in line for. We've given it to Ms Black. Now, there may be more promotions in the future, but I can't say when. I'm sorry, Reaper, but with your carelessness, you brought this on yourself. You'll continue to work in Natural Deaths.'

I put the receiver down very gently and smiled.

Maybe you think I'm letting myself off the hook, but there was a kind of roundabout justice in that, and maybe – just maybe – all this happened for a reason.

Because what if it had been an ordinary day where no extraordinary choices had to be made – no snail, babysitter or neighbour deaths? Thanks to me, in a funny way (funny peculiar, definitely not funny ha-ha) Dad wasn't going to be pushed into Misadventures, which I knew he'd hate and which would make him miserable. Nasty building-site accidents, avalanches, hot-air balloon disasters – that would never be Dad's cup of tea. No. Natural Deaths is much better. As I knew first-hand – by my own hand – it was quick, gentle, painless. So easy a kid could do it. Even a cat.

Chapter 17

Later that evening, we sat at the kitchen table, eating chocolate biscuits. Me, Dad, Mum and Hetty.

Now this is a rare thing indeed, because chocolate is banned from our house by Mum, who says the family should abide by The Happy Husk first rule of healthy eating: *put goodness in to get the best out*. And in this case, for once, she wasn't talking about going to the loo. I think she was talking about energy.

None of us had any energy left after the day we'd just had. After trying to tempt us to fruit 'n' fungus flapjacks Mum eventually gave in to Dad's suggestion of something a little sweeter. We had to close our eyes as he pretended to magic the biscuits out of thin air (although I knew he'd actually just nipped to his secret stash – and I also knew, from Hetty's frozen moment, that she knew all about that too). But we gasped and cheered as if it was real magic. I knew it was just a trick known as Deception.

This was a special occasion, Mum said, and we deserved it. She even had a chocolate digestive herself. Then another and another. In fact, she went through several of them in one go, her lips licking faster than a cat in a delicatessen.

'The one thing bothering me,' Hetty said, giving herself 'face art' with the melted chocolate on her fingers, 'is that we spent all this time hunting for Mr Darcy when we don't even know who owns him.'

'Doesn't mean he wasn't lost,' I said, trying to help.

'So where is he now?'

'I took him home, Hetty, and that's the end of the story,' Dad said in a way that meant 'let's drop the conversation'.

'So you *do* know who owns him.'

'Er, yes.'

'Who?'

'The woman at number twelve, isn't it, darling?' Mum said, staring pointedly at Dad.

'Nope,' said Hetty, shaking her head. 'Number twelve is allergic to animals. I know that because I knocked on her door asking if she wanted to donate to my Save the Pony Fund and she said how she wished she could ride horses, but she's allergic to all animals.'

I knew Hetty's *Save* the Pony Fund was actually a *Save Up* for a Pony Fund. I don't know how she gets away with it!

'And I know Mr Darcy doesn't live anywhere near us because I have asked everyone in the road what animals they own – you know, to break the ice before I ask them for money.'

I saw Mum and Dad exchange a look.

Hetty had never made things this difficult before. And now she was looking at us with her arms folded, a chocolatey expression set on her face. She wanted an explanation.

'Jim, would you just help me with something in the living room?' Mum said, wiggling her eyebrows.

Oh. I see.

I followed Mum out of the kitchen. We stood in the hallway and waited. *Hetty*, I thought, *given a choice, would you rather forget all*

about it or be bugged forever by a question
that no one would answer properly?

Actually, I knew that what Dad was about to do was more for our sake than Hetty's. Because when Hetty gets her teeth into something, she rarely lets go. A bit like someone else I know. I let myself think about her a little before I put it out of my mind.

Fiona would have followed me to the ends of the Earth for that One-Touch, and I'd have probably let her. But although I was still feeling a little warm and fuzzy from all the unexpected attention, I knew it wasn't real. Fiona was like a dog who followed you because you had treats, or like a snail that crawled towards you because you had lettuce stuck to your arm. Her adoration wasn't for me at all.

'Hey, Jimble.' Hetty sauntered out of the kitchen, a little dozy. Dad's hands were on her shoulders, making sure she walked the right way. 'I'm going to bed now. Will you play Warrior Fashion Catwalk with me tomorrow?'

'I have to help Will with his snail-saving campaign, but after that I will. I promise.'

'Good,' she nodded sleepily. 'Oh, and, Jim. If you had to die, would you rather . . .' She paused to take an enormous yawn and Dad steered her right past me and up the stairs to bed. It had been a long day, even by Hetty's standards. I stopped and thought about my marvellous mischievous little sister, who knew right from the beginning that making any choice was a bit of a gamble. Especially when death was involved.

Dad came back downstairs a relaxed man. He took me in his arms, and Mum came and wrapped hers around both of us.

'Anyone in the mood for an episode or two of *Mr Bean*?' Dad said eagerly.

Mum yawned and said she was going to bed. I was tired too – and quite honestly, it was a day I wanted to be over. But Dad looked disappointed, and I figured that it was the least I could do.

'I'll watch with you, Dad,' I said.

'Excellent.' He beamed. And I hadn't seen a smile that big on Dad's face since the *Mr Bean* Christmas special, where Mr Bean gets a turkey stuck on his head. 'Although perhaps we should let the cats out of the car?'

I gasped. I'd forgotten about them.

After we'd let the tide of cross cats loose, we fell into the sofa and sighed at the same time. A sigh that said all was right with the world again.

Hetty crept into my bed in the middle of the night, as she sometimes does. She and Bo-Bo, her bedraggled sleep toy.

'Jimble,' she whispered loudly in my ear. 'Are you awake?'

'Well, I am now, seeing as you just kicked me in the unmentionables with your foot, Hetty.'

'I have a question for you. If you had to live forever on an island or live for a week on top of a very tall spike, what would you choose?'

'Why are these life choices instead of death choices?' I yawned.

'I'm bored of death.'

'Alright, forever on an island.'

'Are you sure about that?'

'No. You can't be sure of anything, Hetty. Unless it's maths, there's no such thing as a straightforward answer.'

Hetty sighed with satisfaction. 'I knew you'd learn one day, Jimble.' Then she kicked me in the unmentionables once more and fell into a deep sleep.

Hetty's crazy games always taught me something, and this time was no different. Sometimes when you think you know what's going on, you actually don't have a clue. For instance:

1) I didn't know that my wanting a *Percy Jackson* DVD would turn the day into an adventure of *Percy Jackson* proportions!
2) Hetty didn't know that by giving me a death choice for a snail she caused me to kill the babysitter.
3) Dad didn't know that by thinking he'd done something terrible, he'd actually narrowly avoided a promotion to Misadventures.

You see, when you're making a decision, pretty sure you know how things will turn out –

BAM! – other stuff gets in the way and suddenly everything changes direction. Life is full of that twisty-turny stuff.

Most twisty-turny stuff is out of our control, but there is something you can do to make it a bit less chaotic. And that's to keep things simple and as sticky-free as possible. In my case, that meant avoiding curiosity-related accidents – particularly those involving death. And to tell the truth. And not to meddle. It was a big call, but if I could stick to the straight and narrow then the road ahead might be a little less crazy, for me and for Dad. And I'd do anything for Dad.

From now on, living with Death was going to be easy.

Acknowledgements

Huge thanks to my patient friends and family, to the talented Jamie Littler and to my lovely agent, Alice Williams. And to you, Matilda Johnson, wherever you are. Thumbs up to Jason Childs aka @Toy_Consultant for his smoothie inspiration. Last but not least, big love to my adventurous readers – you're all absolutely magico!

Rachel Delahaye got told off for talking in class quite a lot. That's because she loves words. After studying linguistics in Wales, very near a town called Llanfairpwllgwyngyllgogerychwy-drobwllllantysiliogogogoch (which is a great word), she began a career in print journalism. Nowadays, when she's not playing Boggle, Scrabble or Balderdash, she writes children's books.

Jamie Littler is an award-winning illustrator/doodler-type person who is the creator of the comic series *Cogg and Sprokit* which was serialised in the *Phoenix* comic. When not busy trying to find all of the pens and pencils he's lost, he spends his time illustrating many different children's books, which have included the world-renowned *Famous Five* by Enid Blyton. He finds this the most splendid and outrageously fantastic job in the world (and yes, he is aware of ostrich racing).

Have you read the first two
books in the Jim Reaper Series?

JIM
REAPER
Son of Grim

'Hilarious and
fun and spooky
and brilliant!'
Pamela
Butchart

Rachel Delahaye

Illustrated by Jamie Littler

Piccadilly
PRESS

Thank you for choosing a Piccadilly Press book.

If you would like to know more about our
authors, our books or if you'd just like to know
what we're up to, you can find us online.

www.piccadillypress.co.uk

You can also find us on:

We hope to see you soon!